WIT... N

D1463688

DATE DUE

MAY 0 9 2008			

T33762

STORIES

UKE RIVERS DELIVERS

R. T. SMITH

LOUISIANA STATE UNIVERSITY PRESS
BATON ROUGE

Published by Louisiana State University Press
Copyright © 2006 by R. T. Smith
All rights reserved
Manufactured in the United States of America

An LSU Press Paperback Original
First printing

Designer: Barbara Neely Bourgoyne
Typeface: Adobe Minion Pro
Printer and binder:

Library of Congress Cataloging-in-Publication Data
Smith, R. T.
  Uke rivers delivers : stories / R. T. Smith.
      p. cm. — (Yellow shoe fiction)
   ISBN-13: 978-0-8071-3187-9 (pbk. : alk. paper)
   ISBN-10: 0-8071-3187-3 (pbk. : alk. paper)
   I. Title.
PS3569.M537914U54 2007
813'.54—dc22
                          2006018761

The paper in this book meets the guidelines for
permanence and durability of the Committee on
Production Guidelines for Book Longevity of the
Council on Library Resources. ∞

To Sarah Kennedy, her inexhaustible grace

They're hardly divisible, sir—well, I can do you blood and love without the rhetoric, and I can do you blood and rhetoric without the love, and I can do you all three concurrent and consecutive, but I can't do you love and rhetoric without the blood. Blood is compulsory—they're all blood, you see.

—Stoppard's PLAYER in *Rosencrantz and Guildenstern Are Dead*

Jesus wept.

—John 11:35

Contents

UKE RIVERS DELIVERS

Jesus Wept

When lightning strikes the outhouse it is anointed. Haloed and shaken and char-dark, it is God-glad but not set aflame like the overhang mulberry tree, and from that day it always smells like buttermilk and dead roses. We call it the Light House now and offer up our prayers there because Daddy is full-circle converted. He has nailed up the dump hole and propped in the seat of a '64 Dodge pickup. We keep a Testament on a shelf where the scroll paper was, but the black book ain't much use, as anybody with their mind on the holy can feel the scripture scorched into the boards. That's what Daddy says. The quarter-moon slot in the spruce door lets sunlight bleed in, but it's God Redeeming that makes every splinter glow. That's where Daddy's shout sermons come to him in a startle, so he should know. He also has hung up a half-moon hubcap losing chrome, which he says is rusting toward the outline of the Jesus face with its crown of thorns. We'll see.

"We" is my Daddy John Crow Epps and my brother Jester. Also myself, Dock. There was never any symptoms of flight in our family before, but now Daddy, whose black hair made him Crow, hardly scuffs the ground when he steps. He's that lifted.

I wish Jester and me could rise up and float about, too. We have to work the sunflower rows on normal legs while Daddy preaches around or witnesses down at Sentry Park or some close-by camp meeting. When the spirit is on him, Daddy hot-wires the possum-colored rattletrap truck and is gone most all day.

It is not so easy for a pair of boys thirteen and twelve to run a flower farm alone. We have to stake some and string them, have to cut the suckers and cull the puny, spray against the aphids, whiteflies and Apollo moths. They are also prone to rust and mildew, so we boys hover close to home, doctoring plants, killing bugs, staying all sweaty and weary while the Word is spread far and wide. Every day here this summer we have to choose what goes to market with El Louise Swofford, who stops by everybody's house who has a whisper crop. The cotton folks with big spreads by the river have their own rigs, and we gawk them whizzing down Governor Toombs Road, which since the lightning Daddy says we should call Miracle Way. When Uncle Pre asks Daddy do you call yourself farming, he says just a whisper. So that's us.

Even Jester knows the short bus El Louise drives is for the lame and halt, but in midmorning she totes beans and peaches, salt hams and yellow vegetables, red peppers, some foodstuffs in hulls, some tasseled. Eggs, too, and sometimes chickens. For us it's just bouquet sunflowers and a few scuppernongs when they come ripe. We do all right.

El Louise is a hefty woman with cigarettes, using state gas to haul produce and fill her pocket. Her hair is hived up tall. I say, Jes, let's catch some wasps on sticky paper and fill a poke. We'll set them in the bottom of a scuppernong basket and see will they escape out to mess with El Louise. Jester says Our Savior wouldn't. He has been in the Light House too often to suit me, so I play-slap him and run off giggling into the crown rows of King Red Streaks. I know I'm marked out to be more responsible, but it's hard.

Our mother hails from Woolwine, Virginia. She first came down here for Bessie Tift Women's College over in Forsyth, and I reckon she was happy once, but everything started going to the dogs a couple years back. Then she didn't take to the Lord setting up shop in the piddlepoop shack. From the day of the lightning bolt, she was sour and riled, sat half the day just gazing out at flash-by highway traffic. Wasn't much go left in her, but Mama and Daddy took to scuffling even worse come evenings. Seems people can always manage to spat.

I don't know what he sold, the Hudson man with travel cases and slick-looking eyes like a cold sky, but she climbed in with her lima-green valise at dusk about six weeks back and was gone in a swirl of dust. Not so much as a word.

Back before his being washed in the Lamb when I guess Daddy used to smack her on the sly, I'd see Mama's face red as a blister burn, arms bruised church purple and gold. One night I was up to spill my water on the yard, where I was salting a dandelion to death, and I saw her in the kitchen working the blue pump by the sink. It has a curved handle which seems like it's too beautiful to be a tool, and three-in-one keeps its iron parts from owl-screeching. I always love to watch that pump work. On that particular night the water gushed out silver, and I tell Jester about what I saw when she stepped clear of shadow, her whole back and shoulders that yellow of a new bruise dawning.

Jester's so riled he says we'll have to kill him, but two weeks later we're still plotting—lye soup, cottonmouth or a coal-oil jacket?—when the storm blazes and the Light House is born. Not long after, she rescues herself in the Hudson.

Now Daddy is down at Jesus Wept Chapel thumping the pulpit against hell-bound sinners and unworthy women. He says plagues are coming, monsters about to be unleashed. He says there will come a swarm of wee-vils and a flood or maybe no rain ever again and sand whirled into a deadly rose. God has told him there will be suffering and gnashing of teeth and bloody sores. They all amen and raise up a hand. They writhe about shouting kaluja! or yes, my shepherd and pass the plate with a flannel pancake in the bottom to hush the coins.

We have eaten our egg sandwiches and shucked our gloves in the shade. I am poking at a chinch bug hole with my weed. Jester has made a creel of wild grapevine and put his wood soldier doll inside with a swaddle dishrag.

Lookee. Moses in the bullbushes, he says, all innocent in the face.

It makes me slap at him again and stomp his Bible story into a mess. I just do some things. I don't know why.

Daddy comes back still cloud-walking from his Jeremiah trance, in-toning on Og the king of Bashan and such, and wants to look at the Blue Horse notebook where I keep receipts from El Louise and all the run-ning figures—profit and loss, halfs and carryovers, spend-outs and owed. The White Owl cigar box hiding sunflower money sits under the rolltop amongst the cubbyholes and pigeon slots with a mess of bill papers. He says money is the root of evil and keeps a mummy-dried bat on top of the bills to warn off any man-jack with selfish notions. Daddy says God Himself needs cash in a steady river to further the Work, but I know he is drinking it. I found an empty Ancient Age bottle in the Dodge springs. It had the old smell all right, and I've seen other signs. Even if he has us get up with the rooster and 'cite the Green Pasture Psalm with him on his knees like some good deacon, he is deep into what Mama used to call "the medicine." It don't speak well for religion, I don't care if he can walk on air.

We stack them in a wagon, careful not to bend the ray petals. Jester sloshes the cut stems till we can tote them back to the cooling cans. Even the shy Brownies and Oxblood brand look like somebody's faces. Some are bright lionheads with star-point manes. Some are just beaming children. Daddy says Jesus is a sun god. You have to respect their joyful no-noise of soft color. They follow the sun's path and are all helio-something-or-other, the Silverleaf and Primrose, Icarus and Evening Sun, the Ring of Fire and other soaring solos, as well as the polyheads like little Tom Thumb, which are yellow as store-bought butter. I don't see myself why anybody with such plants like the Eye of God over six flat acres should need a Light House.

What I want is a baseball, a crate of co-colas, one ride on the Ferris, a little pet birch tree so its bark will hold onto light from the moon. A deep well and good furrows ain't enough to keep a chap like me smiling forever. I've got calluses on my fingers and lots of nicks. My shoulders stay slump-sore, and the stalks make an itch burn, but Daddy says just to use bag balm at night. I'd enjoy to have a beagle pup and a glass-top showcase for my arrowheads. A bullwhip to crack at rats. Jester wants a *Have Gun Will Travel* cowboy kit with the sideways horse head and some floss candy on a stick. We both want a book of fairy stories and a bike. Pan of fried chicken. Daddy says we are pagans. Remember the poor, he says, the miseried and starving. We should be ashamed.

It is after dinner, and we are sick of souse and butterbeans, boiled okra, collard greens, hopping john that tastes like mush, pone cakes, tomatoes and Luzianne water with no sweetening. It's our mama's cooking we yearn after. Fried drumsticks and pies, the sunflower loaf with blackstrap and fig bits. She could make a chicken that would put manna in the shade. He says we're ungrateful and stomps out. Says we are heathens who wouldn't be happy with ginger beer and butterfly pie, says we are the kind that drove the nails in and stuck the spear.

Clean 'em up, Epps, no idle hands, choppy-chop! He means the vittle dishes. The vein in his right temple is a blue snake.

Now he's holed up in the Light House again, most likely with a pocket bottle, whipping up a new scare-'em sermon to reap any stray dollars that might happen along. He stamps and raises his voice in the holy closet. I would like to see the lightning come back and miracle again, so I am listening hard for thunder booms, but now all I hear is his tambourine bottlecaps shivering like a rattlesnake, mad.

Then one night he catches Jester peeing in the washtub, and we have to start trailing along to Jesus Wept to get our lesson in Good. Spending so much time pew-cramped and dozing upright, it's hard to keep the farm on calendar, and some flowers are stooping, begging any Samaritan passerby to cut a bunch. Shirking work: Is that what they mean by revival? We should feel lucky to get the rest, but I'm antsy. Pretty soon we'll need to start barning the runts and other wounded flowers. About Christmas we'll sell the seeds for bird snacks and roasting, the worst mealy ones for sow mix. But only Daddy has the trained eye for what we pour into the press and crank the handle to make helio oil. He read the flower book cover to cover by himself and has been in it since before Jester was born. Before that it was dusty goobers, which will stoop a man bad and have no self beauty. Sunflowers were his plan to make Mama happy, a pretty crop against all the dirt and bland, but now he is just a prophet and a lily of the field. Me and Jes'd need to learn for ourselves how to press the oil, if there was enough time we weren't down at the chapel. Daddy is worshiping us straight to ruin.

Then Daddy brings home a sulky gal from Macon, says we should make her welcome. Pandy Cleave. She is a natural slattern—tassel blonde out of a bottle, a long jaw, eyes gray as gravel and can't cook any better than me, but she has a Sears guitar, which is the beat of a tambourine any day. Now me and Jes get to stay home and do our job again. She sulls around the house and is no use, paints her nails and writes silly songs, and after supper it's jibber-jabber, jibber-jabber, jibber. He-dove and she-dove, coo and coo.

Jester says Daddy thinks he can save anybody he wants. That man ain't got the sense God gave a goat. I'd get a hiding if he knew I said that, or most anything that crosses my mouth when he's out Bible-beating. We're trying to get used to her, but she favors those peculiar old Carter Family songs ands sings "The Storms of Jordan" tangled up with a murder ballad about Blackie. Me and Jester know better, as we had the plum-colored Philco, but I think Hudson Man thiefed it off. We didn't miss it for days, but who else?

It all comes to a head now, like a boil on your scruff. Pretty soon it's the middle of August and she ain't adding to the work crew or giving much help in the kitchen. Just lazing. Daddy says she'll gallop on down to Jesus Wept fast as a thirsty jennet on the day when the Holy Ghost surprises her, but till then she can just hang about and be what he calls available. The Holy Ghost is like something in a wedding dress you can't quite see. It will jump you from behind. That's why there's no point looking out for it. I wonder would she hear the call if it to come.

I already don't trust her. Things she does. Pandy thinks it's fun to sneak up on most anybody, but she creeped behind me once in the coop and made me drop a handful of Dominecker eggs where they smashed and ran, three useless suns.

Mess with me and I'll cut you. I have it out already, bright with the morning's fifty stone strokes. Daddy said a dull knife ain't no knife at all.

I'll tell John Crow, and he'll whup the tar out of you.

You won't tell him a thing. My eyes and the Barlow give her every reason to believe. Gleam.

But she has a hanker to fool with Jester. I don't know it yet, but then I do. We are in the hillside rows, cutting a bunch of glory circles for a cash windfall order from the Senoia Methodists, and I am trying to daydream butterfly pie. It must taste like slap-happy colors with sugar, food in a dream. A wind is breathing, and a hawk goes over, his X sky-sweeping over the leaning rows. Then Jester behind me breaks out crying and says Hell might be coming for him.

You never done nothing worth notice.

The harlot has me.

I can see tears streaking the dirt on his cheeks. Talk sense, Jes. What?

He tells me Pandy has taken to touching him on the gizmo. It started when she was washing him like pretending to be our mama, tickling him till he got all wiggly and his gizmo swelled up a bit. He couldn't stop it. She got him once when Daddy and me were cleaning the seed press and once when I'm in front, trying a cigarette and haggling with El, and

Daddy's as usual out Lording somewhere. Broad daylight. Now he's afraid to go into the Light House.

He says, I thought she wanted to cuddle like a mama. She has a sweetness in her voice. You know that blue train-yodel she has like Jimmie Rodgers. I was took in, and she gives me pennies. Now I can feel the devil crawling on my skin. He reaches into his coverall bib and brings out a clutch of coppers.

I be damn. I'm about to explode, but I don't hit him. I hold it in, knowing who's to blame. Then I say we need to get something else on her. We need to blacken her name.

For three evenings we give off work early and use the tall stalks of Gold Giants to hide our way back. We are like Crocketts—field edge to the crepe myrtles, run run run, the abelia shrub where our Joshua cat likes to doze, then up to the house, flat as shadows on the board and batten. Inside the front door I can see his coat peg is empty, so she's alone, like usual. No Sears Roebuck music. No supper sizzling. I don't know what she does all day. Then the third evening we find out.

She's in Daddy's and her room at the rolltop, so Jester fetches the hubcap, and he's on my shoulders, reflecting through the window. I know the room is mirrored up funny in the chrome, but he can make her out and motions me to set him down.

Pandy's got the books, and she's changing my figures with a pencil rubber. She has the old Owl cigar box. Dock, he whispers, she is filching our cash. It's on her lap over the rose-print dress. I think she is robbing us. The bat is on the floor.

We crouch there and figure. She can't make letters like me. Nobody can, as I write a peculiar tilty hand and cipher a lot on the edges. How's she going to fool John Crow Epps?

She'll get caught, Dock. He won't let her. He won't keep her on if she's a pilfer. Anybody can see that. Could she really be that stupid?

Not for long.

What we don't know is she's got a scissor-lock on him. That's what Uncle Brinson used to call it. Her night work has smoked his judgment. I find out when I try to tell him, and what I get is the wrath side of God's message, the back of a hand. Blood leaking out my nose.

You've got your mama's demon in you, boy. You're a born heathen. If there's flower money missing, I'll know who to look to. That vein again, beating.

He storms out and walks to the yard swing, where she is looking at the moon. Pretty soon they are giggling and drinking from a sack. It don't occur to him to ask where she got cigarettes and a fresh hair ribbon. Jester and me lie abed and wonder how to bring him back to solid ground. We toss about and scheme till their spring squeak comes under our door and through the walls with their moaning, but then sleep swallows us up, and then it's time to perk coffee and hit the fields. I hear her in the back bedroom strumming chords while she pops her gum, and the Ford truck is gone. I don't know if he's told her I have borne witness. I don't much care.

While I make us lunch buckets Jester taps the table in time with the coffee spurting up into its little glass bubble, bibbity-bobbity-boo.

We have a hard day, Jes, lots of bunches to tote over, and a sight of watering.

I know, D, I know, but I don't care for it now. I can't understand. Why do we have to work while Daddy plays Jesus? It's the Light House's fault, that's what it is.

I say, Don't forget your round hat. I can feel a scorcher coming.

When we trot down the steps, I can hear there's no noise from hers and Daddy's room. I would like to see her chewed and spit out by God. Daddy says it's a rule not to suffer a witch to live, but he wouldn't know a witch if she was cackling and stirring afterbirth and rabbit crap in a kettle.

It's a rough one all right, a brain-burner, and we have split hoses and a slow sputtery pump to work with. The pump at the field heart ain't a patch on the blue kitchen one, and we have to ram a hoe handle in so we can work it together, sucking the water from a deep spring nobody has ever seen. At the spit head I have some stripped threads to fight with on a joining. The way the pipe wrench opens its jaws puts me in mind of the Godzilla, and that's my idea of God, I think, chomping up the doers of evil, even if it means you-know-who in my own family tree.

We break off to load for El Louise, and she grins like a gator handing me a big fold of money to settle for the month. I stuff it in my bib so we can get back to what Daddy calls appointed toil.

Like always, I eventually get some thread cuts from twisting on new pipe steel, and like I say, it's a rough one. By noon I see Jester is flagging on me, so we take our tea water and biscuits with black bananas and boiled eggs in the shade of the flowers. I love to stretch on my back and look where the sky is blocked out by our giants. We have some tree helios out of rogue seeds, the blooms bigger than our straw hats. It's like sunflowers are your army of mighty shields. You could almost believe yourself safe from anything in the sky down here, like the world can't find you. The highway is zooming by, but I can't see it. It can't see me, neither.

Jester has got into poison oak and is scratching like a flea terrier, so we head back to the house for calamine, but when we get there, something feels wrong. I holler for Pandy, but no answer. Then it's up the steps and through the house calling her name. It's just an echo like a hollow log, and I'm not surprised much, but I know where to go, and sure as Judas, there's the cigar box and bat on the bed, not a dollar in sight. I'm in a frazzle. If he thinks it was me, he'll be dangerous as a runaway cropduster. Still, I don't have much choice. Where would we go?

I tell Jester, and it sinks the heart out of both of us. We chip ice and make big glasses of water to sit on the porch swing and watch for cars and trucks passing. He'll be home, we reckon, in time for something to eat. We sit quiet as bird eggs. The Bible says for everything there's a season, but I'm not ready.

When he comes, he bounds out the truck cab again smiling and giving out hosannah. I can see he's got that air-walking gait again, but I hold up the box. All gone, I say. She's done struck out.

She what? She what? The vein swelling.

He gets red as a pickled beet and, snort-breathing, runs inside shouting her name. He must be thinking: just like Mama. His usual angle of wrong.

Now he runs out the back and around the sheds yelling no-words and also screaming he has been touched by the she-devil. Jester and me just sit there, nothing else to do. She has loosed all the sins and horrors on the world. We just hope he won't turn it on us.

Then he's back in the house again, throwing fury fits, pounding walls and snarling, kicking chairs and stuff about. Fling and hurl. The flatiron comes out a window, and me and Jester decide to get some distance. The smashing and splintering is like a twister has set down in the house, so we drag the ladder over and climb up top of the roof, where it might be some safer. Pull the ladder up, just in case. We are still in the frazzle. We want to be calm, but we're too scared.

When he comes out, he has his daddy's war pistol and is raving, Heathens and pagans, anathema the bitch scourge of God. Kneel with me, sons, he says. Kneel and raise our mighty plea. We crouch down and don't feel too safe, but he looks up at us perching and says, Boys I'll bring her back, I'll get our money, I'll smite and venge, o abomination, and a laugh like somebody plain crazy.

Then he is in the truck and gunning the engine. Coming to the road, he stops like deciding east or west. It's west, and we watch him heading after the sun that's going down like the king of the flowers. He leaves a swirling trail of rusty dust. From up here I can see our thousands of flowers in their careful rows, holes where the cut ones are missing, lanes for the sprinkler that's spitting water feeble like a cricket. Out beyond, our crops—the acres of flowers waving, refreshed—give way to Mr. Popwell's sweet corn ready for its last picking and then the Forney brothers' soybeans still growing. Farmhouses, yards and the road seem like they're glowing till everything in every direction just blurs with twilight and the worn-out day's haze.

Jes is slowly turning, shading his eyes like an Arapaho scout, other hand still scratching.

Do you reckon we'll see him again, Dock?

Come sleet, come gray wind, the world turning like it does, I expect he'll show up with his tail tucked. Maybe he'll come back wrung out, unsmitten, whole. If he don't show, we'll keep the farm ourselves, if we can.

Before long we figure it's safe and run the ladder back over the edge.

There's no weather clouds flocking up there, so I halt my steps on a middle rung and say up to my brother, I have me an idea. Let's torch the Light House and be done with it. Kerosene in the barn. We'll say lightning again if John Crow Epps comes back. I don't care one way or the other. I've got eighty dollars in my chest pocket, and we've got a heap of orders.

Then Jes says, Can we have fried dinner now, D? Can we sacrifice a chicken?

Pagans like us, you know. Jesus wept. I lock my eyes on a fox-colored hen, and we climb on down.

I Have Lost My Right

When we heard the horse we moved from the firelight by the ivied oak where we'd been bivouacked and stood to our mounts. It was coming right at us. Pistol aimed at the snapping brush, I called out a challenge. Virg was crouched beside me, his hackles stiff and fangs bared. Haemon Willis and Coates had their Sharps at the ready. Nobody was our friend; we couldn't be too careful.

"Name your Jesus or get misery and oblivion." I cocked the hammer.

"Gentlemen, my Jesus is the roaring boy Jeff Davis," the voice came back. "I smelled your smoke."

He could've been the worst foe, might've been our nightmare, and we couldn't chase him off to go back and reveal us. We had to know. "Approach and be recognized. Come slowly, stranger."

The rider emerged from the copse astride a huge chunk of a horse, wide as a wagon, and Coates called out, "What in the black hell is that? Looks like you could have the whole Trojan army stowed in that thing."

I didn't like Coates. He was cross-eyed and ornery. I didn't trust his resolve, but I was stuck with him.

"It's a Morgan. My own sweet Caesar took some shrapnel down by Wilderness Church. I had to put him down, and this monster was standing, drinking from the narrows of Scott's Run. He'd dragged a sledge with a man on it. That unlucky Christian must have caught some frightful lead. His head was all caved in, what's left looking like a cherry cake. I'm Reeves Eason. Captain. I've been riding around all evening with these dispatches, and I am altogether spent. Do you gents mind if I unlimber?"

An officer, but his outfit and accent were the right color to match ours, so we stood down and offered him a cup of rye coffee. At least he wasn't a danger right off, but Virg still acted cautious, slinking around the workhorse, which paid him no mind and started tearing new grass.

Eason swung down from the stirrups and wrapped the strap of his pouch around the pommel a couple more loops.

"Some mastiff you have there. He wears his muscles like an acrobat."

"He's a dragon on people he don't take to. Who you with?"

"A courier out of Old Jack's staff."

"You with him when he got popped?"

"As it happens, fate assigned me that sad vantage. The night was black as the inside of a polecat, just a glint of moon. Boswell was reaching me a map when the idiots volleyed. He snapped to attention, said, 'Lordy,' and dropped stone dead. I think Old Jack was just hit in the hand, but then Little Sorrel ran him at the flashes. He got bucked about and branch-lashed across the eyes. Another round and the general was hit bad, finally snagged tight in the bitter fortunes of war."

Here he paused and squatted on his heels like a countryman.

"It should have all been over before that. We had the bluebellies fooled. We hit them at Talley's, at Dowdall Farm. Hazel Grove was an error, but we recovered. We knew the terrain, and we had their right flank in the jaws, enfilading fire; we were rolling them up. But then it got dark, and that was pure bedlam, skirmishers blazing away in all directions, taking down their own people. That was why he chose to scout it, to discover the right conclusion in person."

"We heard they took his wing, but he's strong and sure to come back riled."

"That's the current story. They're moving him to Guinea Station to rest up. Hunter McGuire is a keen doctor, smart as a whip, no nonsense. Put him under the laudanum. They say Jack dreamed music while they sawed him. It was the sorrow song of blade on bone. Might as well be our anthem now. I see by your caps you're from the Two Corps, Barton's. What mission are you pursuing so far off your unit?"

That was the one we were dreading, but we had a story. The confusion that made it easy for us to slip off was an excuse for most anything. Willis was the one who worked it out, who suggested we should give the whole show up and go home. With the fiery brains of the Stonewall Brigade out of action, he figured the end was coming, and I reckoned why not get back and put in some corn, instead of learning up close what a northern stockade was like. Besides, I had one of those premonitions after Sharpsburg. That was the longest, reddest day I ever wish to witness. It was looking like the generals was working a contract to exterminate us all, and I'd commenced to believe "skulk" means "save your bacon." I wanted to go home and start over, live inside my dream of a regular farm life—sow and gather and grow old.

So I said, "Tell you the truth, we don't know. We were scouting up the Salem Church Road when Hooker swung his batteries. That was holy hell, worst I've seen. When the brimstone was over, Kyd Douglas sent a batch of us with intelligence to Early. I reckon you heard how that turned out. We were too late and met Dan Sickles coming on from Fredericksburg. Some blue horse-boys chased us for the better part of a day, like they thought we had some big secret. Everything that favored a path just vanished in the brush and hardwoods, and we was lost in the tangle. I was praying for a God sign, but it was Virg, this dog, that showed us through the Wilderness and back here. We're hoping to hook up with Douglas and the other scouts come first light."

We was hunkered down now about the fire, warming our hands on the sludge we were calling coffee, wishing words could make it so. The dog was pacing on the shore side of the tree, alert but not nervous, making little half-circles about that big horse. Virg kept sniffing the wind and cocking his head. Wasn't any other sounds but the stream slipping by— branch of the Rappahannock, we reckoned—and every so often an owl off to the north.

That captain didn't seem at ease. With red piping on the breast and pants, his uniform was good quality, a real contrast to our shoddy, and he'd give a tug here and there to make it snug neater on him. He wore a brace of big navy Colts in his belt, and he was a little soft-faced, I thought, young, but with old eyes. Everybody had old eyes by then. Still, I was sure he had somewhere else he wanted to be. In the darkness, with no flags and no generals, he seemed a man who might still believe in glorious war, but maybe it was just the same fear of being afraid we all felt.

"You ever knowed Old Jack up close?" Willis asked.

"On occasion. I have seen him close enough to know to be wary, but near him is sometimes a good place to be. I remember last Christmas we were bivouacked not too far from here, near as I can reckon, and I helped serve up a dinner at the Corbin house. Jimmie Smith, his orderly, had commandeered turkeys and white biscuit, a bucket of oysters, pie and wine pickles. Stuart was there in his ostrich hat, and General Jackson dandled a girl child on his knee."

"And what did you get?"

"A drumstick to myself and pone and a slough of beans. A warm cot, a lullaby instead of "Taps," a safe place to shit. That whole Moss Neck time was halcyon, but even when he was cooing at that child, he scared me."

"How come?"

"Don't get me wrong; I reverence Old Jack, but he's got killer's eyes, and with all that Bible zeal mustered behind them, they seem a peril. I can't get over how cold they can be, like they're looking at you from the moon. But the boys love him, they do, and if we ever have to figure out how to fight this crusade without him, well, I'm not convinced we could manage."

It was Coates' turn, and he took out of his mouth the sweetgum switch he'd been chewing.

"I heard what he said at Fredericksburg about the Yankees charging on the wall."

"What was that?"

"General said, or they say he did, 'Shoot them all. I do not wish them to be brave.'"

"That a fact?"

"They tell it for true. Name's Hob Coates. I mustered into the Rockbridge Artillery with Jimmie Smith in '61. Didn't know the old boy'd got himself on the easy wagon. Staff, by damn. We had us some serious times together, riding the caisson or swabbing a cannon by day, talking sad about home at the campfire. Likely the war's got to be a lark to him now."

I didn't like where this was going, so I said, "Coates, this hell ain't a lark for no soul. Boys started off with braid on their hats and shiny swords found out loving Minnie was no honeymoon."

The officer spooned some of our beans and sowbelly into his pan and asked, "Loving Minnie?"

"You know, the Minié ball, song of the death angel, like a banjo string snapping."

"Yeah. You don't have to be at Bloody Lane to testify to that," said Willis. He was shuffling about the scrag for dead sticks.

Coates kept going. "I knowed the general in Lexington, too. I mean, just to see. He wasn't no personality to speak of. Just a haughty professor kind of fellow. The VMI cadets said he . . . hush. Listen." His face had gone hard as a Choctaw mask.

At first we heard nothing, then the rattle of tack and gear clanging up-wind on the road. Then we went into a quiet scurry. We got the fire covered with dirt from the pit and went to our horses to cover their nostrils. I was worried that clodhopper Morgan would whinny, afraid I wouldn't see my thirty acres or Luanne and Junebug again. It could be Federal scouts feeling out our lines or a straggle of graybacks aiming to reconnect with Lee. Even bummers. Either way, we was dead for sure if they got wind of us. I thought about Jack's officer, about his not really knowing what you might call "our predicament." I touched the handle of my Bowie knife. I could feel the antler bone, rough in the dark. For ten minutes that seemed an hour there was nothing but the soft damp of Hector's nostrils and the tar of night and that sanded antler bone, my palm going back and forth across it, my mind thinking of cutting the new man's throat quick, just to narrow the possibilities. I was drifting loose, everything I believe in turning to dust, all my secret plans falling away, trying not to think of home, the rich dirt, my old daddy's voice. I reckoned if we got caught, it would serve us right, but I wasn't on right's side anymore. We had crossed into the Valley of the Shadow on our own steam.

I noticed the dog was leaning against me, his hackles sharped, muzzle thrust into the darkness. I knew his black lip was curled, excitement dripping from his tongue. I could feel him tensed like a bowstring, and I prayed he wouldn't get a wild hair. In the year he'd been with me, his instincts had proved right every time I could judge. Hoping he'd stay smart, I was holding my breath almost past possibility.

Then the moon came out of a cloud, and we could see some. Just woods, the clear space over running water.

Then somebody whispered, "Didn't hear us, didn't see."

"Was it Yanks?"

"Don't know," said the officer. "No sense taking a chance. Been enough night mistakes in this battle, everybody half asleep from loading and shooting, loading and shooting and trying to remember a prayer. If we just lay low, morning will set things right."

While Eason was unsaddling and gathering pine limbs to stretch his blanket on, he asked was I from Carolina, on account of my accent. I told him I was from the southside, farm country below Roanoke, so he wasn't far off.

"And you've seen some action?"

"Hot work. Hot and bloody."

The dog was snuffling around him, not studying the horse no more.

"I never seen Virg to take a liking to anybody so quick. He ain't the world's most friendly cur." But sure enough, Virg was nuzzling the captain's hand and licking it. It seemed to make the man nervous.

"We have a pack of Walkers back home," he said. "They're just frisky, like children."

"Where's that, home?"

"Kentucky. Six or so days west from here. Not too terribly far from the Virginia line."

"But your people voted to keep in? Why'd you join with the southerns? I mean, you could as easy be riding with those bluebellies back yonder."

He laughed and said, "We don't know for certain they were Billy Blue, but yes, I suppose I could. And so could Jeff Davis, another son of Kentucky, you might recall. My uncle served with him down in Mexico, Buena Vista, and I appreciate his words. Jeff said that if we're not free to pull out of something we joined, we're not very free in it, either."

Coates caught my eye then.

He finished, "Appears to me people have a right to live the way they want, and if somebody sends an army to change their mind, well, woe betide." He was settling his gear and making a pillow out of his kit. "I believe I'll try to sleep now. If you all will work out the sentry duty, you can wake me when it's my rotation."

He was a peculiar fellow for an officer, and I kept getting the feeling he had things he wasn't saying. I wondered did he really trust us, being as how we were, well . . . it might not have made such easy sense we'd be so misplaced after the fight. Maybe he swallowed our story, maybe didn't, but he did pull his hat over his eyes and lay back like a man who meant to put hisself into our hands. I figured we'd just let him sleep, split the watch between the three of us, and be ready to move come sunup. That was a long time off.

I woke to a general pandemonium, snarl and snuffle, horses snorting, the cries of men in the darkness. A shot monstrous close. Another. Dawn was just getting started, a flitch of bacon in the eastern sky, and I could see Willis was laying across a log, not moving, his face bloody.

It didn't make no sense, what I could see by the firepit. Virg had something he was dragging at, and Eason was smacking him across the back with a pistol. Coates had grappled Eason by the jacket and was trying to pull him away. Then I saw Coates' big stabbing knife move, but the officer twisted out and swung his pistol around and it whoomed right against Coates' belly. His body jumped back, and Eason drew down on me, shouting, "Don't move, don't do it." Virg was ascamper now, dragging something through the briars. He gathered speed and went past me at full skedaddle.

I could see what he had clamped in his jaw was chawed meat and bone. It looked like an arm.

"Call back that damn dog, sir, or I shall open you up."

I was still dazed and sleepy and discombobulated, so I couldn't understand him at first, but he repeated it.

"The dog. Call it back."

I hollered into the woods where ground fog was making the bloomed dogwoods even more ghostly, but I couldn't see hide nor hair of Virg. Then Eason was beside me, and I could see a terror in his eyes.

"We've got to get it back," he said, but then, "No, it will be too late. He is a dog, and the damage is surely done."

Tears were streaking into his sparse beard, and I asked what the hell was going on. He kept the pistol leveled at me as we stared into the woods.

"That was Old Jack's arm the dog stole."

"What're you telling me?"

"The general's arm. Now I must work fast."

It had started when Willis dozed off, and Virg got into the captain's message sack, drawn beyond any discipline he had to the grueful secret that had been luring and taunting him all evening. He must have got it out of the bag and the raincoat it was wrapped in before the noise woke Willis and Eason. Being as it was too dark to see clearly, Willis must have been afraid the commotion meant Eason was turning on us, had found us out for deserters, so he went to kill the man, but his Sharp's just blowed up, ripping off his face and hands. Then Coates rose up and joined the confusion, and that was when I come to. But then, whilst Eason was explaining to me, we heard a horse a-gallop and saw Coates riding west like hell for leather, so he must not have been hit mortal.

"Why did they try to kill me?" he asked.

"But what are you doing with the general's arm that has been cut off?"

He had the pistol, so I told him our sorry story fast as I could, desperate to hear his own answer. Willis was gone to the Kingdom for certain, and I didn't know what would come about next, but I was pretty sure old Coates would not be circling back to look after me.

His story turned out to be right simple, too. The doctor had told him to take the arm into the woods and bury it proper, but Eason knew his chief would likely be up and on his feet in a few days, and like any good Christian would want some say in what happened to his parts. Since Eason had been sent on a scout—it wasn't no dispatches he had at all—he figured he could spend a couple days on a ramble while the army pulled itself together and Jackson come back to his senses, after all the buckeye whisky and chloroforms had done wore off. He was disobeying orders, too, and now didn't have nothing to show for it but a story he might have trouble finding believers for. He had a new look of menace on his face, and I saw he was somebody capable of strange reasons.

I said, "Look here, captain . . . ," and that's when he told me to turn around.

When I woke up that time, I was in dire pain. I was gagged with a stick and rag and tied, hand and feet, and I could see what he'd done. Then Eason was holding a flask in front of my eyes, and I couldn't breathe, couldn't raise spittle, the gag being tight and my body heaving and panting. The fire was burning fierce behind him, and morning was filling the sky. I think I heard some birds calling. I don't remember. The pain was just under my shoulder, and it felt the way lightning looks, all jaggedy and too bright for human gaze. He'd taken the better part of my arm.

"I noticed you favored your left hand, so I took the right one. I used the serrate edge of your hunting knife, and I believe it's a lucky cut, a clean job, considering. I have cauterized it, and when you're pert enough to sit a horse, we'll get you to some corpsmen. I believe you'll fare well enough. Would you take a drink?"

That was when he explained how this bold course had solved both our troubles, because my war was over, and I could go back to the bosom of my family. He tied up his bundle again, and I saw my arm for the last time, disappearing into the bloody rain slicker. All I could think about was the pain and would I live to see my front gate again. Ever so often I would look past the rawhide tight on me to the singed sleeve and my blood showing around my wrapped-up stump, and I would go swoony.

Soon as I was able to sit Hector without everything swirling back to night, we lit out. He didn't bother to throw no earth on poor Willis, and as he had no face, I wondered if he'd get to Heaven, or if anybody would ever know who he was. The crows in the leaves over us wouldn't likely care.

The business went tolerable well back at camp. Considering. The captain told the sentries I was tied onto the horse for my own safety, and they bustled me straight to the sawbones' tent. All the surgeons was amazed at the story. The captain said he'd come in on the hindquarters of a skirmish, and I'd taken a ball near the elbow. Pretty soon Kyd Douglas himself was setting beside me saying I was a bold warrior and a lucky man. That captain was right about some few things: Like so many busted rebels, I was headed home, nobody suspecting I had lit out on my own furlough without waiting for such a hard reason.

But he was wrong about Old Blue Light shaking it off, wanting his pieces back and hitting the Yanks all over again like an avenging angel. The general caught the fevers, I heard later, and tried to move ghost troops to the front in his delirious raving. His wife was there, and everybody saw him fading. He crossed over the dark river in a week. Story is the arm got buried without much ceremony, and I have to wonder didn't they ever notice it was a right arm, and not the one where Jackson took Minié balls on that black night after Chancellorsville. People say there is a marker there and pilgrims still go to it to tear their duds and shed tears over the Lost Cause. I don't expect to make the journey.

I heard once that Reeves Eason saw the wildfire close up outside Gettysburg and did something heroic, following Old Pete this time, but he must have somehow missed catching the devil's eye up there by that graveyard in Pennsylvania, because ten years after Appomattox I got this short letter from Richmond on fancy stationery paper, and all it said was, "Did you ever find that dog?"

Docent

Good afternoon, ladies and gentlemen from hither and yon, and welcome to the Lee Chapel on the campus of historic Washington and Lee University. My name is Sybil Mildred Clemm Legrand Pascal, and I will be your guide and compass on this somewhat dull, dark and soundless day, as the poet says, in the autumn of the year. You can call me Miss Sibby, and in case you are wondering about my hooped dress of ebony, my weblike hairnet and calf-leather shoes, they are authentic to the period just following the War Between the States, and I will be happy to discuss the cut and fabric of my mourning clothing with any of you fashion-conscious ladies at the end of the tour, which by the way will be concluded in the passageway between the crypt and the museum proper. If anyone should need to avail himself of the running-water facilities, I will indicate their location before you enter the basement displays, and please, all you gentlemen, remove your caps in the chapel, and also, ladies, kindly ask your little darlings to keep a hush on their voices as they would at any shrine. No flash cameras, please, in the General Lee alcove. No smoking, of course, a habit I deplore.

Now, I am sure you know a lot already, and I may cover ground you have heard before, but please respect those who enter this tour with an open heart, and I will periodically pause to entertain questions, though I do not personally see any reason why they would arise.

The Lee Chapel, built on a Victorian design with intricately milled brick, was completed in 1868, during the General's tenure, but it wore no green gown of ivy to begin with; I myself adore the ivy and do not care for the recent decision to trim it back. At this time of the afternoon it turns the light attractively spectral, wouldn't you agree? And I do not believe ivy could rip the building down. The chapel, which has never been officially consecrated by a legitimate denomination, should not be confused with the Robert E. Lee Episcopal Church, which you can see at the end of the paved walk with the steeple facing Washington Street. I am told there are two Episcopal churches in the world not named for saints, but that is not one of them, which is told locally as a joke, if you think such things are funny.

If you look directly above to the bell tower, you will see the black face and white numbers of the timepiece, which with its chimes duplicates the Westminster Clock in London and is dedicated to the memory of Livingston Waddell Houston, a student drowned in the North River, though I do not recall when nor deem it important. The pendulum, of course, is invisible, as in all the best devices. The numerals, you will notice, are not normal American ones with curves and circles but the I's and X's and V's of Latin, a language that was taught here to the young men from the beginning and still is to some few, especially those who wish to stand for the bar. Did you know that the "Lex" in "Lexington" is Latin for "law"? I have heard, however, that the young ladies who have matriculated—it's been some dozen years now since that inflection—do not enroll in dead languages. They are here, no doubt, for progress, and do not have the time to spare for such niceties. If such a perspective keeps them provided for and protected, they truly have my envy. In just ten minutes the hour will strike and we will hear the tintinnabulation of the bells. I love that sound and will not abide random chatter once it begins.

As we proceed through the front portals, you will see on either side caracole staircases with bentwood banisters, and we will file to the left, but mind you do not cross the velvet ropes to climb the steps because insurance issues must guide our path. We are entering a National Historic Landmark that is also a museum and a tomb, and especially in these troubled modern times, we must show the greatest respect. Perhaps we could say the very existence of this edifice—which is, as I say, a National Historic Landmark—is one of the rare benefits of that old and storied war, but watch your step: We do not want to add you to the already lamentable casualty count.

As we enter the vestibule, please do us the kindness of signing our guest register, which bears the autographs of presidents and princes, as well as luminaries from Reynolds Price to Burt Reynolds, Maya Lin the memorial designer to Rosalynn Carter, Woodrow Wilson, Bing Crosby, Vincent Price and the Dalai Lama. Fifty thousand visitors annually, I believe, many of them repeaters from far and away, devotees of Lee, people who love the Stars and Bars or have a morbid curiosity, I suppose, about the Fall of the South. If you have a morbid curiosity about the Fall of the South, which is not the same as a healthy historical interest, please save your comments for your own diaries and private conversations. One of my cardinal epigrams, which I will pen myself someday under the title "Miss Sibby Says," is this: "History is not gossip; opinion is seldom truth."

I am sure many of you all know as much about General Lee as I do, but because some of the information you know might be false, I will highlight selected facts as we file through the antechamber and into what one is tempted to call "the sanctuary" but is actually only a multipurpose auditorium, though a splendid and clean one. You could eat off the floor. When the General, who was indeed a legend but hardly a myth, agreed to come here as president, right after the sorrows and fury of the war that rent our land in half and wasted a gallant generation, he did so because, as he said, Virginia now needs all her sons, though there were fewer than forty students enrolled at the time. This chamber will seat six hundred, so we know he had a vision. He was a military man with many projects and plans, "strategies" they call them, and I was once betrothed to just such a disciplined and tactical gentleman myself, but fate has denied me actual wedlock, among other joys. If you have been denied a significant portion of life's joys and your own prospects, you will indeed understand.

The school, of course, was then called Washington College and had been spared from Yankee fire in the end by that revered influence and the statue of dear George atop the cupola of the main building on the colonnade, which always sounds too much like "cannonade" to suit my ear. We all wish that our dear Virginia Military Institute had been similarly spared, but alas, invaders have their own designs. Many people such as foragers and raiders can come into a place as easily as into a person's life and leave matters far more damaged than they found them, for they have their own designs.

And please do not hesitate to touch the pews or try them out. If you'll kindly look at the wall to your left, you will see the engraved plaque testifying that the General, whom some students wanted to call President Lee, which you must admit has a nice ring to it, sat here during services, though he often napped, accustomed as he was to catching a few winks on campaign. A man who has marched and fought as a steady diet for years will find civilian life a difficult fit, and General Lee was no exception, though it was in his ancient blood, as genealogical experts have proved that he was descended from Robert the Bruce through the Spottiswoodes, though far more honorable than one Spottiswoode descendant, whom discretion prevents me from calling by his sullied name.

I daresay some of you have served your states and countries and may have posed for portraits like the two flanking the memorial gate. On the left you see the father of our country depicted on the grounds of Mount Vernon, and you will no doubt note that the Virginia Militia uniform he wears so handsomely looks English, complete with gorget and musket, for he fought for the German Hanover English kings against French and Indian savagery, though he would later alter his opinion of the French. You can see he is a young man, confident and noble, even a touch haughty, with marching orders in his pocket, and the sky behind him is overcast (like both today's sky and the current political climate), but there is a ray of light unsuppressed, and we can all hope to witness that ourselves someday. This is not to say that every officer who encamps, lays siege, then suddenly debouches is acting on official orders, for some are not to be trusted.

Before we ascend the steps and cross the stage to examine the second but primary portrait, the image of the most trustworthy man imaginable, I should inform you that this chapel has been renovated and expanded on several occasions and was almost razed in 1919 by no less fifth-column a foe than the college's own postwar president-of-the-moment, a man named Smith, supposedly, who claimed it was a firetrap with a perilous heating system and a roof that leaked like a war-worn tent, though despite today's threatening weather, you should not be alarmed. He had designs of his own and wished to replace it with a huge Georgian structure, but the Mary Custis Chapter of the United Daughters of the Confederacy, in which I am still proud to claim emerita membership, entered the fray, along with the Colonial Dames and the DAR, until the renovation party was vanquished, the field secured and the site declared a shrine. My own relations were in the vanguard of this action, which may bring to your mind the question of my personal role as docent, which is a word that used to mean "professor," though I am surely not one of those types. A docent is a hostess, a volunteer, like so many of our martyred sons. I like to think of my function as an older sister who opens the door to hidden history. "Decent" is the closest word, and decency is what I strive for daily, despite personal disappointments. My own fiancé never felt such hospitality was a function an unattached lady should perform, but since his furtive departure, I have done what I please and have risen through the ranks of a somewhat special and discreet society called the Keepers of the Magnolia, who are dedicated to preservation of the past. In France the magnolia flowers are called *les fleurs du mal,* and we Keepers have appointed ourselves sentries against the invasion of evil revisionist history and the casting of shadows over past glories. The battalions of blasphemers come in my dreams whenever I can manage to sleep, the unholy reunderstanders and condescenders, and they may wear the masks of scholars but are no better than carrion rats, their tails scratching the hardwood till I wake up mouthing a silent scream.

This space is now employed by the university for a variety of programs and gatherings, since as I said it is not an actual church, and the atmosphere of holiness depends entirely upon who is present. And now you and I are here and can add our reverence to the general fund. In the past few months we have hosted six weddings (all of which I have attended in my docent attire), one somewhat tipsy Irish poet and our own famous alumnus Tom Wolfe the Pundit, dressed in a French vanilla ice cream suit and spats while speaking of the death of art. We have heard the angry opinions of Mr. Spike Lee (no relation, of course), tapped our feet to the Armenian guitar band right after a forum on cultural diversity. We have been entertained by near-president Al Gore, and just yesterday the community witnessed the famous celebrity Dr. Maya Angelou in a headdress like a parrot and with a mighty voice, but you no doubt are eager to get back to the more historical highlights of our tour.

Yes, Pine's portrait here is the original, and the family said it was lifelike and true to their father's features, perhaps around the time of the Wilderness, though it was painted thirty years after his death on that chilling and killing October day from what some say was a stroke, and if he was in fact the victim of foul play, as I myself have sometimes suspected, no evidence has surfaced in all this time, but he was a strong man and a good one, younger than I am now, not old enough to succumb easily to the natural shocks that flesh is heir to, if you'll pardon me. He used no spirits or nicotine and had always displayed a flirtatious vigor, though Mary Chesnut's diaries remark that he was "so cold and quiet and grand" as a young man. No doubt he felt already the inconvenient weight of destiny, and she, as I remember, was blind to some species of charm. Yet if he was in fact the subject of knavery, no verifiable evidence has ever surfaced, though there was no official investigation, which should itself arouse our suspicions. We know the northern press reviled him, and more than once public sentiment in the victorious states was roused toward trying him for treason and marching him straight to the gallows. So great a man cannot but beget enemies. I am certain you have known of plots yourself to undo the virtuous and lay waste to their peace of mind. Some men smile and smile and are villains, as the poet says. When the General breathed his last, the rain came down in torrents for days in a loud, tumultuous shouting sound, and flash floods were widespread and ruinous.

Few are aware that the General's birthday, January 19, coincides with that of Edgar Allan Poe, who represents perhaps the dark side of our Virginia psyche. Fewer still realize that the General's extended family's loveliest estate was not Arlington, which was his wife's Custis dowry, but Ravensworth. If that connection is not enough to lend this chamber a chill, I ask you to imagine that perhaps Mr. Poe's "Annabel Lee" in fact concerns a young lady from a family the poet could only aspire to. The cosmic inequities of romance abound. A sad prospect, but we may only ponder it and move on.

Above the wrought-iron gate is the Lee family crest with its Latin motto *Ne incautus futuri,* which means not without regard for the future, a valuable reminder to those who would dance light-hearted till dawn rather than consider the demands of the morrow. My favorite detail is the squirrel rampant and feeding above the argent helm, which reminds us of those animals' foraging and storage, their self-sufficient happy chatter and industry, though Lee himself in no way resembled a vermin creature. He was five feet eleven and every inch a king.

The centerpiece, of course, here under the various regimental Stars and Bars, is this recumbent statue, carved from a single block of Vermont marble by Edward Valentine—truly his name, according to sources, but deceit abounds. He was said to be from Richmond, where I came out as a debutante farther back than any of you can possibly remember, and I believe it is the rival of any statuary in Italy, where I have always hoped someday to visit, though I was long ago disappointed in my best opportunity. And strong as the temptation may be, please do not touch the statue, for any mortal contact would mar the surface of the stone, which is like the magnolia blossom itself. Have you ever touched a petal and watched it rust before your eyes? Precious things are the most vulnerable, for the slightest blemish can destroy. Could that be why we are most devoted to what must perish?

I would like to direct your attention to the texture Mr. Valentine's chisel has given his campaign blanket, the soft-leather look of his boots, the elegant beard, but please, I repeat, do not touch the statue, for the living hand with its native oils will soil this chiseled stone. Our touch could not now warm him, and see how at peace he appears, in complete repose? He looks, in this muted light, serene at last. He at once is and is not a "touchstone," but if you bend your ear closely, you can almost hear the beating of his hidden heart.

Mrs. Lee instructed that her beloved be depicted napping before an engagement, sword at his side, gauntlets nearby. He is not to be considered dead, but only resting, and there are some who claim that he might yet rise, might return when the Commonwealth needs him most, though his actual remains are located in the crypt beneath the stairs. Doesn't that word "crypt" remind you of the writings of Mr. Poe? It means a secret code. This chapel is not, as you may have surmised, a structure without its own secrets.

Do you recall Mr. Disney's charming film *Snow White*? Since first I saw the princess in her trance I have thought of the General as someone under an enchantment, awaiting the right deliverer, but perhaps it is the trumpet of the Second Coming for which he waits. And no, I do not for a moment believe, as one rude visitor from Florida implied, that his effigy resembles a large salt lick that animals might tongue down to nothing. The very suggestion disgusts me. He could never under any circumstances be nothing and was present even when not in attendance. Mrs. Lee was herself chair-bound and grew accustomed to his absence. She endured three sad years of widow-weeping after his untimely passing but at last found the peace of oblivion. It is perhaps a peace we should not underestimate.

As you know, General Lee could never sleep in a bed after Appomattox, for he was haunted by the many gallant men he had led to the grave. In fact, who is to say that he ever truly left the war, as he wore his gray coat and campaign hat with a military cord until that October day when he succumbed. It would not surprise me if he did not sometimes see the students as his troopers and Lexington as beleaguered Richmond in miniature, considering his stern correctness and the martial bearing he never abandoned. He wore the dignity of conflict to the end. His last words were, "Strike the tent."

Be careful as you descend the staircase. You will pass the vault itself, which is carved into the bowels of the earth like a dungeon, with its many Lees walled in, from the rogue Lighthorse Harry to his sons and grandsons, and you can see the diagram of his family tree with its fabled roots deep in the richest Virginia soil. Mrs. Lee herself is there behind the bricks, and so outspoken was her love of cats, one can only speculate whether some feline remains can be found there as well. Other relatives have been unearthed from the cemeteries where they were first invested and transported here in high ceremony, which is enough to make a mere mortal's skin crawl, but you will appreciate how important it was that they all come home.

Before I leave you to wander the gallery with its pistols and portraits, documents and costumes, his office as he left it with maps and papers, his veteran Bible and the massive but eloquent correspondence that he sustained like a man still issuing orders, I would like—well, yes, I must remember to direct you to the restrooms yonder and the gift shop where you might purchase postcards, keychains, paperweights, bracelet charms, videos and other keepsakes. You will no doubt desire a souvenir of this visit. As you pass his desk, I suggest you speculate on what momentous documents hide there before our eyes, in plain sight. It was there he wrote the college honor code and there he penned his personal motto—"Misfortune nobly borne is fortune," a code I always strive to honor and embody.

And please do not forget to express your generosity in the contribution box, for though there is no charge for admission, the chapel does not sustain and clean itself like some haunted mansion, but rather requires our vigilant assistance. So long as we can generate donations this shrine is one cause that will not be lost.

There is time here on the threshold for one last morsel of history from Miss Sibby, the story of Traveller, the noble steed who is finally interred outside the lower exit. What an astonishing narrative his is. He was born in 1857 and named—amazingly—Jeff Davis, then purchased in 1862 by the General, who renamed his mount after Washington's favorite stallion. He carried his master through the entire war and then to Lexington, where they were close companions, often making the jaunt to the mineral waters of Rockbridge Baths. Some evenings the General could think of nothing but the mud and gunfire, the broken bodies of young men, the twisted faces of the wounded and weevils in the meal, and on those occasions he would excuse himself from table and walk out to Traveller's stall, run his burdened hands down the muzzle and brushed mane of his boon companion, then step out to the garden to relieve himself in starlight, listening for ghosts, looking heavenward and weeping. "It is all my fault," he repeated after the bloodbath of Gettysburg, for he was not one to dodge responsibility like some I might name.

Traveller marched solemnly at the funeral with boots reversed in his stirrups and lived until 1871, at which time he stepped on a rusty nail and died of lockjaw, which also strikes me as a little difficult to believe. He was himself a symbol of the South's pride and beauty, and therefore had many enemies. Death loves a shining mark, and he was buried unceremoniously in a ravine cut by Woods Creek, but his amazing journey had just begun. Raised from the grave in 1875 by the Daughters, his bones were sent away for preservation, but an inexplicable red hue had infused them, and there was no turning them white. In 1907 the skeleton was returned and mounted in the museum, where the students who had earlier plucked souvenir strands from his tail—well, not those students, obviously, but later ones of the same ilk—circulated the word that academic success was ensured by carving one's initials upon the bones like sailors making scrimshaw. In a less harmful jest, a buck goat's bones were once smuggled into the museum, assembled beside the General's steed and accompanied by the label "Traveller as a colt." You cannot ever guess what boys will think of next, even after they rise to manhood and begin to sow promises like seeds, or pebbles that resemble seeds but yield no living issue.

Beside the door you will see Traveller's memorial stone, which is even in this cold time of year decorated by visitors with coins and candy, apples and miniature battle flags. It is a place for wishing and the site I linger at when my day here is finished and I am waiting for evening to embrace me.

If you should care to pose any questions about the General and his highborn kinsmen, his four maiden daughters or his influence on the liberal curriculum, I would be pleased to address them now, though I have decided it no longer prudent to speculate on what the General would have thought about admitting females to the college or what his ghost might have to tell us about his sudden postwar decline or what he made of the works of the scandalous and ill-fated Mr. Poe, who also attended West Point, but was more *bête noire* than *noblesse oblige*.

Now I must leave you, for the security guard there with the evil-looking eye has taken it upon himself to restrict my tours to the chapel proper, which is why I at once savor and regret the fact that it has never been consecrated as a church. If you do not choose to rendezvous at the monument to equestrian fidelity, I thank you for your interest and kind attention to our sepulchral treasure as well as your indulgence of an old woman's eccentric ways. I bid you, now, at this charmed threshold, a fond and wistful adieu.

Tube Rose

The last evening I saw Granny Annie she was rocking in wicker, the whole porch creaking with the weight of her grief. The neighbors and relatives had eaten and gossiped and gone, leaving their plates and tumblers and stains all over the house, their condolences trailing behind them like coon tails on aerials, and the flower wreaths were wilting on the grave.

"I can't believe my William is gone." She was rocking and weeping in cadence, swallowing the dregs from her Sun Drop and fiddling with the snuff tin in her lap. I could see by her eyes reflecting the yellow bug light that she was mustering up a song.

"Don't sing."

I'd been living there all summer, doing for them as she sat by Pappy Will's bed stroking his hand, soothing his brow. I would water the Big Boys, milk the lame cow Ho Boss and collect in the eggs. I would slop the half-dozen hogs. She would hum and whisper and get herself ready for the end. We had a pact: I would chore, she would not sing.

It wasn't that she couldn't. Lord, but her voice was a wonder, a gift, an affliction. As Pappy Will grew sicker, she slowly lost the reins that used to keep the beauty one step ahead of the possible peril. When she tremoloed or colored a note, the wall paint glowed, the water pipes shuddered and Butch the redbone howled. If she reversed a chord or slung the key to a flat, spiders called back their webs and flour rose from the cracks in the kitchen's pecanwood planks. I could hear the wires in the upright Baldwin tighten like a hundred crossbows.

I had been just a chap in the Young Apostle pew down at Gospel Wind Chapel when she last sang in public. It was April of '47, her soprano rising above the choir's cage of harmony like a bird of prey. The air filled with the smell of burnt matches, and the infants bawled. Everybody said the hair on their necks hackled up, and the pages of Brother Webbern's Bible fluttered back and forth like a whirlwind had taken them. The hymnbooks got too hot to hold, while the Baptist banner split its silk. Then the doors swung open and a mighty gust shook through. Even after she stopped and the choir opened their eyes again, it took a couple minutes for the laws of nature to collect themselves. Right then everybody said, "That's it; enough is enough."

I would scatter cluck corn and toss hay, feed Butch and the tiger cat. I would hull the peas and grease the tractor axles. She would tend his miseries; she would not sing.

That last night, though, I could see that after the strain of holding her tongue at the funeral she was wavering, and I did understand. Just fourteen, I already knew the way a wrecked heart can torture its host human.

We had tried to avoid breaking down by keeping our summer habits. Every evening after Pappy Will's sleep dope, Granny Annie and I would sit sentry on the porch and drink our sodas. I was Dr Pepper; she was Sun Drop. Dishes done, his last suffering words of the evening faded into the bedclothes and curtains, the vaporizer misting Vick's into the room, we'd go out and strive to behave like the hale and unstricken. I'd read in *Lee's Lieutenants* or Tom Swift. She'd crochet or flip through Uncle Sugg's *Upper Room*. Not being Methodist, she wouldn't read but scattered paragraphs, shaking her head. And she'd dip snuff.

That was the great mystery to me: how her voice could be so rich and unsettlingly holy when she measured out the rusty-looking stuff on her birch spoon and stowed it behind her lip. She could drink that pee-colored Sun Drop while she did it. She could even talk pretty clear, and she could sing, though she promised not to.

Sometimes we'd have the radio in the front parlor turned up to listen to *Gospel Jamboree* over the nighthawks and crickets. Some rant-revivalist would be citing scripture or saying, "Repent tonight or pay the fiery price," and they'd pause for her commercial as fireflies Morse-flashed around the abelia. Twangy studio singers would croon, "If your snuff's too strong it's wrong, get Tube Rose, mild Tube Rose. You'll feel much better all day long with Tube Rose, mild Tube Rose." She'd smile and say "That's a fact" and bend over to spit a stream of ambeer into the cess of her can. I had to look away.

It was always a blue Planter's peanut tin, and I had come to hate them. Mr. Goober was always dancing a jolly little jig with his cane outstretched and monocle shining. He wore spats and a top hat like the owner of Mac-Donough's Funeral Home down on Hulett Street, and his pitty skin was almost the same nutmeg yellow as the snuff powder, not to mention the color of the World War I Battle Atlas that Pappy Will kept on the wall of his office where he went to smoke and clean his nickel-plated pistol. I knew his old uniform growing dirt-dauber apartments in the closet kept that color, but the buttons were the gold of Camel tobacco flakes on his lip. It was all the color of cancer to me, and Mr. Goober came jigging across my dreams more nights than one, his grin like a snake's. I would not eat a peanut for love nor money.

Cotton across the road was glowing in the moonlight like furrows of snow. I could hear a mosquito zipping and unzipping the air around me, all hypnotic-like, in spite of there being no rainpools they could hatch in. I sipped my cold drink and hoped the whip-poor-wills out in the privet would not commence, for it was the one temptation I knew she wouldn't be able to resist in her grief-shock. When I thought I heard the first one, I blew a round alto note across the bottle mouth to hide it, but her rocker ceased creaking, and I could hear her listening.

Then another whip-poor-will, the three most mournful notes in the world, the shiver in that last syllable the edge of all the mortal sorrow we're born to. The birds pulled the dark around them and sought succor from memories too dark to have names.

"He is out there singing to me. William is. He's lonely and cold. I can't deny him."

I could feel the chill running down my spine while she was still inhaling, getting her lungs full of woe and country air.

"Silver threads and golden needles cannot mend this heart of mine."

I couldn't stop her. Over and over she breathed out the same sentence, sometimes giving it a chant solemnness, other times dirging it or switching to a glee-club sparkiness. I was touched by it, the many tones of her spellbound stillness, nothing moving in the world but her vocal cords and bellows, but I was also scared, then terror-shaken. The mosquito at my ear dropped dead on the puncheon. The yard willow began to sway like warning of a mighty storm. Soon the rim of the sky began to glow yellow like there was a distant battle, and the corn, well, its tassels all sizzled and gave off smoke. I could hear muscadines popping in the arbor, as the weathercock spun and the rusty old screen four feet from my face commenced to glow violet and tremble. The peanut can on the hassock tumped over, spilled its Styx River onto the floor, then rolled toward the trapdoor to the root cellar, and her voice had grown into a ripping howl.

I didn't want to touch her or get closer, but I knew I had to. "Granny," I shouted into her ear, "Granny, you've got to quit it before we're killed."

When she turned her eyes at me, they were burning like she'd seen something out there beyond the beyonds. They were red as Hell's handles, and nearly about popping free of the sockets. Next thing she did was whistle the three tones of the lonesome bird—"whip-poor-will"—and they were so right, so eerie and animal and invading, that we both froze. I wanted to reach out, to soothe or shake her, to remind her of the peril she might deliver us to, but then she stood up from the rocker and pointed both her hands at me like a craving angel. As she struggled to step closer, she shivered and stumbled and went down like a sack of hammers. The porch shook, and the pillars groaned like the Last Days were upon us.

Five minutes later I had her covered with a blanket, her head on the chair cushion, and I was scrambling under the settle bed for my straw hat and duffel. I was heading out. I wanted to see morning from another county, and my daddy could come back from his war and the icy Inchon if he wanted her looked after any further. It didn't matter a hare's whisker to me if the road was dark and the color of snuff under my fierce feet. I was leaving the land of miracles behind and hoping for rain before the peach trees withered and even the distant cities I had only vaguely heard of were chastened and smitten with flame.

Trousseau

As it was quite dark in the tent, I picked up what I supposed to be my "raglan," a water-proof, light overcoat, without sleeves; it was subsequently found to be my wife's, so very like my own. . . .
    —JEFFERSON FINIS DAVIS, 1881

He was forced into the ultimate position of cowardice; he was a man who hid behind women's skirts, most literally—a man who denied his biological destiny and donned women's clothing.
    —PROFESSOR NANCY BERCAW, 1997

We will hang Jeff Davis from a sour apple tree. . . .
    —Union marching song

His old discipline served him well. His clothes, even if threadbare, were "well-fitting, refined," and "scrupulously clean" and neat.
    —FELICITY ALLEN in *Jefferson Davis: Unconquerable Heart*

The train clamored and shook as the jagged landscape of Appalachian twilight ghosted by. Grandfather stared at his reflection in the window, stroked his beard and said:

He was not attempting to deceive anyone, my boy, not one soul. The Yankee press—hounds on a blood trail—reported him fleeing disguised in woman's attire and called him coward, but Jeff Davis had not a white feather in his wing. That devil Nast cartooned him as a frocked and bonneted frigate, but we know mischief will ever eclipse truth unless someone step forth to correct the caitiff lies. Jeff was no nance and not even deigning to evade his fate but headed to Mexico to gather loyal forces in the West. He was a tornado seeking fresh wind, new music, a safe place to regroup and contrive. Why, even northern memoirs record he wore on that day "a waterproof and brass spurs of unusual size." But the victors have penned our history in bile, made the noble cause seem the mischief of ghosts, and they are followed by apologists who weakly protest: "Only his wife's raincoat, only a tossed-on shawl against inclement weather." Such dodges are little improvement over the scurrilous lies.

The truth is, son, he was both a fierce warrior and a private cross-dresser, no catamite or bend sinister but a genuine ram who just loved the touch of rust silk faille or taffeta with ruched sleeves and chain lace. He savored the rustle of a train, the feel of pleats and plackets and darts, the intricacies of bustle bows, hooks and buttons. Even the roughest soldier understands the lure of satin on the skin, the need for relief. Even the hardest Spartan loved to spruce and primp. Remember the hot gates of Thermopylae. I loved him for that, as well as martial conduct and caparison, but not in carnal ways. He was our inspiration, a haggard man, a besieged cavalier, a pariah, still equal to any king of Thebes.

With your dear grandmother now at rest and the boatman Charon glaring me in the eye nightly, I see it's time. I owe you this story. If I could offer it up as a ballad and blend my voice once more with good Jim Speed, it would make more sense. You'd feel the weight. Jim had a sturdy voice and had run the barges on Big Mississippi till news of Manassas stirred him. A lanky Tennessean, he showed me camp cooking and how to mend a rip, how to make weed coffee and allow for elevation discrepancies in a downhill shot.

Before we were mustered in for Jeff's protection, still pickets outside Fredericksburg, a volley from the dark tumbled us into a shell crater where we prayed and cringed till birdsong coaxed the dawn. It was winter, '63, and we sprawled there silent, clenching our pain while our blood seeped and mingled. We shared hard prayers and solemn vows, gave up our secrets freely. In first light I noticed the marvel of his eyes that went darker when he pondered things, as if a bird flew through them and left its shadow behind. After that night of horror and hardship, we were as one, sharing our short rations or a soiled dove in Miss Winnie's Dixie House. Jim Speed. Now that was a man.

Truths and rumors knot and snarl. It was raining like Noah's last warning on the night of the capture, but we had been retreating stealthy through Georgia for days. The treasury gold had been dispatched west to confuse our pursuers, and the president's family achieved the plotted rendezvous at last. Splash and splatter: Weather came in torrents and ran through our shelters. I was riding vedette and hating both mud and the dull raingear over my finery, the brushed livery of a palace guard. The first redbugs of the year were itching me, and my horse was testy. We still believed we might drown Pharaoh's army in a sea of red.

I should briefly digress. The landscape we had passed through was war-ravaged—collapsed barns, fields run rife, black snaggle of foundations still smoking while sheds already hosted wild grape and ivy. The air was active with insects and pollen, deerflies big as robins. The spoiling corpses of horses stenched from their ditches.

Even the back roads were thronged with refugees, both white and dark, moving in whatever direction might distance them from carnage, carrying whatever they could haul. The aspect of defeat lay upon every pilgrim, from the ancient mammy to the trunk-burdened blueblood in rags, the cracker child in ripped plaid or skulker in mufti. Such sad spectacle tempted us to set the spur and flee the sight, but we aimed to be gentlemen, to avoid driving them to the bramble with our mounts and wagons, and as we waved, some bared their heads or gestured back, though others scowled or spat in our wake.

As we pressed deeper south and into the vernal season, flowers exploded from their stalks, and songbirds brighter than fire paused scarce long enough for us to pass. Then the torrent commenced. Noble Jim had rendered his cloak to a young soldier crutching on a single leg, and I shivered to see him drenched. He was a man who strove never to display his pain. The world will not see his kind again.

It is fact that our commander was wearing female attire when they netted him, but not some haphazard raglan slicker. As I recall the evening— and decades of merchandising have sharpened my discerning eye—he emerged from the tent in leaf-green taffeta with curved back seams, an artful gown gathered at the weskit with clear seed beads as embellishment along the tulip bodice. It was an outfit I had long admired, but topped by a plain countrywoman's bonnet, to shield his face from weather. He had just lit a cheroot and lifted a stirrup cup of brandy to the future. Jeff was weary but much relieved to be back with his family, and you could see the Crusader gleam residing in his good eye. The mischief that got him court-martialed at The Point, the adventure of camels for the cavalry, the sorties at Buena Vista—they were lurking still, despite his sharpness, his quarrels with Congress and six secretaries of war. We got our surprise then—it was the initial instance we understood that Miss Varina must have been party to the Confederacy's closet secret all along. He was dressed for the ball and beaming. She stood at his side, all smiles.

It soothed him to costume and make believe, you see. It helped him plot sorties and calculate supply routes or enfilade, but the sound of gunfire and scrimmaging dragoons, as ever, lured him that morning, and he was looking for his navy Colts—as John Hammond reported—when he saw the Michigan freebooter spurring his nag over Cake Creek. The hour was dark as a skillet, and stumbling, he ripped the skirts away to free his movement. The Black Hawk War had taught him the trick of throwing a rider by lifting a foot from the stirrup, and that was Jeff's intent, but Miss Varina caught up and threw herself between them as the Yankee was cocking his carbine.

Personally, I believe the weapon might have misfired in the downpour, and Davis would have swung onto the horse and away, bold as Bedford Forrest. Such was his courage that we might yet be a Confederate nation to-day, but his dear wife, like Pocahontas, intervened. That spelled the end of our odyssey for freedom, our sovereign dream. As you know he lived into his eighties, broken by chains and a close guard, pardoned later but less citizen than penitent, until resurrected as a martyr. Wherever he traveled, defeated people scattered whole Edens of roses at his feet. I wish I had seen it. The papers reported he held his predator's edge like a falcon in jesses.

Bless his memory, but you must wonder how chance brought a mild clothier like your grandsire to serve as witness to such history. It had little to do with chance, for I was not always this broken crow you see before you. Now listen close.

After years of warring I was still hot for a fight that morning, my blood up since we'd crossed the Ocmulgee at a skirmish site where the uniforms of our fallen were hung like ghosts from the sycamores. Anyone could have seen that I loved our Cause and leader. I was riding with my boon companion Jim Speed and nearly fearless. My breath was quick, face red-appled. I was ready for butcher's labor. We had escorted him and guarded, served and conferred, polished and preened with our great captain, stood at attention and slept in our boots and kepis, but close duty hemmed up in Richmond had kept us from a soldier's proper rage. For two years we had not seen a big scrap without a spyglass, and though we had become darlings with charm and delicate palates, as well as a fine eye for millinery, we could still drill a target, put the spurs to a flank, our mounts foamy and snarling, the raised saber lovely as the new April moon.

But we did yet have our state secret, and no one kept it half so *sub rosa* as Jim Speed and I. Dear heaven, even in this new century I miss him, poor Jim of the walnut skin and honeymoon smile. His cheekbones were Cherokee, surely, deny it as he might. His hair was a raven's shocking shade. He was among our last true heroes and a wizard with a seaming needle or flatiron. His deer eyes haunt me still. . . . But such a secret. We had a pact, renewed it nightly after taps. We would never betray the masquerade.

Of course, our recruitment to the president's personal guard had required some doing, some smooth allure, as we were mostly country boys and more ripe for mending hames and larding axles than some sartorial cult. In Richmond at first we'd romp and rollick on our furloughs while the Federals slogged about in the peninsula's gumbo mud, taking heavy losses, changing field marshals ring-a-rosy as poor citizens ripped up fences for kindling, the shivering prisoners on Belle Isle moaned and anchored shackles in the slave market rimed with frost.

We'd sample the local bumbo and fall into cribs with doxies we would never greet on the daylit promenade. The air was filled with desperate festival, garish signs and tease shows, damaged humanity begging in the alleyways with their banjos and mule-hide tambourines. Such is the aura of siege, and gaslights gave it an infernal gleam, while the rumble of hearses kept the rhythm grim. I'd pick on the mandolin and sing bawdy tunes as Jim whittled wood scraps. He could make deer and mallard stroll forth from a chunk of oak or cherry, but I entreated him to carve demon faces and fright masks. Pent-up soldiers are the first to wax strange.

Then Jeff called us into his chamber, the inner sanctum of books and flags and presentation sabers. I was nervous to shivering, but Jim stood calm as Jack's cat, and Jeff's text was the matter of manners, but what a speech, running from whisper to plea to pulpit thrill. We'd need to learn the gestures of high society to move at his side, to shield him in close quarters. Spies abounded, he said. Sometimes, when he went abroad in disguise, one of us would have to accompany him in the outfit of a matron—convenient, for all the frocks and bother afforded ample space for weaponry. That was why we scraped our chins, despite the style *du monde*, to adapt the skirt and demure demeanor. Jeff's goatee should have been sheared as well, that he could more easily slip through definitions, but the satyr in him would not agree. Samson on his mind, he adopted the widow's veil. I laugh now at how astonished I was at that first summons just to be standing on a carpet from the Persias. I had so much to learn.

Even now my fingers tremble to think how Granny Lee would have blushed and burned to know his old Mexican brother-in-arms had adjusted to lady's foundations, how he smiled to rouge those hollow cheeks and paint himself for phantom cotillions, to take tea or sherry all genteel and formal with his eight praetorians, we dolls of rebeldom laced tight in Chinese silks and smuggled satins as we sat circled in his chamber strong as Round Table knights, rehearsing polite society. It was all the odder as most of the natural belles were by then clothed in mourning, but we would map battles over demitasse and discuss rail routes with our pastry. And money, always pondering the problem of money and choked trade. The treasury was a ripped feedsack leaking.

We also had our inner mysteries, which are now of little interest, but know this, child, as the planet spins and stars bivouac above: It is not unmanly to address the Eve in your nature, and Jeff Davis, I can testify, contrived his wisest strategies thinking with gathered tulle at his wrists and hoops like the orbits of planets encircling him. With charts and compass and calipers he projected troop movements or figured logistics on the back of a shawl pattern. He often pondered dispatches to Lee and Bragg in the field while eyeing his image in the glass. I remember once his dictating a corrective to righteous Stonewall himself while I pinned up a hem. Jeff's suggestion likely saved a corps and mad Jackson's reputation. He summoned great originality to prevent our Cause from being lost.

But you must yearn for a beginning to set this narrative on a less shocking course. Cipher back to see it. I was but eighteen the year after secession spring and still following our nock-eared Jenny. Sixty-two had opened as a world of axes and reap hooks for me, the tumbrel sledge and bucksaw, scorp and froe maul. I had not heard of Shiloh, but word of iron ships dueling in Virginia had reached me, though I could scarce believe my ears. I endeavored to mind my own business, though I was a stout fellow and handy with a musket. Still, I kept with the clodhopper life until that sweaty day wrestling with the bull-tongued plow for a straight furrow despite the mule's limp. She had been snakebit in March but survived because I pressed a split hen to the wound.

Since dawn we had been rough-clearing the bottom for jethro cotton, not meddling in others' business, though Sumter had fallen so long ago, and many enlisted. A few souls were already back home bitter and missing limbs, while the dead list grew, but I strove to think of more local concerns.

The almanac decreed it high time to cut the rows, and my mind was awander, trying to order and wring out my griefs. My father was stroke-stricken and silent by a dead fire gazing at the dream of gentle Jesus in the ash. My dear one had thrown me over for a Charleston indigo factor, a fop twice her years strutting his fancy life on the Battery, in the mansions and banks, a man who could think with a dollar's mind and was turning profit from the national plight. Even a bumpkin could see he was a villain.

What came over me that hot Sunday was the question my Chapel Hill mentors would later trace back to the ancients: How do I change my life and shed this man-weakening urge to weep? How do I hold to the honorable line? I had not yet heard of the Stoics. I knew nothing of Greeks.

I had just turned a sweet pivot at the south end under the bean tree, lifted the share and dressed its sharpness back into rooty dirt, when I saw the odd sparkle. Another three feet of cleaving and I was wading in stones. When I bent over, son, I could see the cantle was all arrowheads and lances, black flint, quartz and chert, all knapped and trimmed for their dark work. Redwings in the cattails screeched. Somewhere an ivory-bill hammered.

It was a marvel to behold, but I had my appointed labor, and the sun does not hold still—seed wants burial under the fresh moon. I gave the *gee* and *haw,* slapped the reins and pushed on, but the soil continued to raise Indian war and hunting, the whole row behind me flashing in the sun. I stopped and took stock, sure this was a crucial moment. Something distant was calling out clear, a voice of duty plain as a trumpet. As some are called to God, I was summoned to the Cause.

That night I slipped out the window and down the road under the year's last wave from Orion. I passed whip-poor-wills calling and found the coach road, striding hard, not looking over my shoulder lest Uncle Carbo cracking a plow line might be gaining. My eyes grew to savor the darkness, as I was finally clear on my destiny. My mind said two things: I would abjure treacherous women forever; I was going to join the war. Half a century has passed now; perhaps I can claim cure. Your dear grandmother—rest her spirit—proved antidote to half my folly.

The war had brought us all deprivation, a diet of rice and turnips and biscuit, while Sandlapper South Carolina was a scab of a land, the remaining residents mostly demons in advanced training. The home front was hard, our blouses thin cotton sacking, our only salt scraped from the smoke-house floor.

My sole refuge had been Melinda Rue Lavelle, who pledged herself to me behind the Berry Church, but when she withdrew all promise in a letter so curt it cut like a neutering knife, I finally understood my home was no more than a wasteland. Even the Cherokees had left. Even the posies were wilting and the dogs shiftless and tattered with mange. Why not go for a soldier? Why not oppose the storm blowing blue and evil from Lincoln's North?

I turned sharp in the direction of Yankee trouble and reached Tar Heel soil, where the roads were flanked with women of all shapes and colors putting in tobacco. Slave coffles trudged in chains. Catalpas bloomed like popped corn, and finches darted about more yellow than silk. Shackled Negroes drove teams at a trot, and some even offered me rides. I saw their attire resembled my own, but their part in the war was a mystery, for I only knew that armies from the world of iron and grimy cities were coming to pillage the land. Still, the dogwoods were in flower, elm and Judas tree as well, while hedge birds sang steady enough to celebrate what many of us, alas, would die to defend.

I almost made Raleigh before a cavalry scout in his scarlet-trimmed uniform and polished gorget told me where to sign on and acquire my own outfit. I can still remember gazing up at him, backlit in the angled evening light, his spurs and buckles like pirate treasure, his worsted trousers clean as a preacher's, waxed mustache like a Shawnee bow. I shaded my eyes to see the bridle and hilt of a cutlass, his brass buttons like small suns. The black boots shone, and above his brimmed hat two feathers from another world caught the smoky wind and shimmered, their pattern a pooling angel's eye. I later discovered a bird called "peacock" was their source, old fable Argus gone local. I collected for years the symbols of allegiance to a doomed Cause's beauty, but pray never allow yourself to succumb to their lure. They are but tokens that took many a sweet lad to his death. Yet I was awestruck by the cavalier's braid, a cord twisted tight as a hangman's rope. He performed a salute and galloped off in the direction of the falling sun. Awe-struck, I followed.

It was all dash and chaos that hour of the infamous capture—no sun, no stars, few lanterns. It was little improvement over the last months in the capital, where gravediggers rattled down the night streets and Binder ordered his scouts to torch the stored whiskys to save the city from riot. Richmond was soon a sprawl of scorch and blaze.

We had traveled so many miles that spring—by train to Danville, where the citizens were cheery despite the shocking news of Appomattox. Days later in Greensboro, the reception was colder: The *hoi polloi* shunned us. There the cabinet met in luxury railroad cars, and I later

heard Secretary Mallory report of one counselor passing resolutions between a bucket of stewed apples and a ham where a Bowie knife stood
like a sun clock's gnomon. Sheer Pandemonium. The generals argued surrender—Glory Beauregard most adamant—but Jeff would have none of
it. Lee, he harangued, was not our last hope, just a reluctant convert who
lost faith. Named the King of Spades that winter (for all the trenching and
graves), Marse Robert had lost some of his appetite for fight. It was April,
though, and Jeff felt his sap on the rise. The fruit trees shook their frills.
Only we few of the circle knew, as he admonished the faint of heart, of
silk knickers and gartered stocking under his presidential garb. Jet-black.
Trussed and constricted, he was spoiling to continue the war.

Soon we heard the rail-splitter was in Richmond, visiting ruins, breathing the smoke. The spy Miss Lew and Bison Botts were running free, rousing rabble, while the streets teemed with freedmen. LaSalle Pickett actually received Yankees in her parlor. The city was charnel, the trees stripped.
Lincoln was seen resting in Jeff's own easy chair. One soldier claimed, "Ape
in his undertaker's stovepipe and broadcloth was perched high on our
Confederate mansion, waving his Old Glory like a madman." Jeff doubted
it, said Lincoln lacked the flair, "but he breaketh the bow and cutteth the
spear in sunder." You should have seen the chief's eyes at that instant.

In Charlotte we learned of the fool Booth's cowardly attack, then heard
a bishop's sermon on resignation and acceptance. Hostilities continued in
pockets, however, for others thought to pursue insurgent war. We pushed
deeper south into the Palmetto State, pursued by three thousand cavalry-
men, desperate to catch Jeff's fleeing family. We drove the horses near
collapse. Always, always, he was agitated and spoke of broadcasting war
like dragon's teeth sharp and ready to rise. "Enemies abound," he told Jim
and me. "We shall never want for targets."

Suddenly he sent the army away, against all advice, which was his
habit. He had secret dispatches. Retreat became flight. His aides John-
ston and Lubbock stayed with us, and we rode on tired horses while the
treasury train headed elsewhere. You can imagine his exhaustion and joy
when we met with Miss Varina near Dublin, Georgia, but the pleasure
was brief. He sometimes rode in her ambulance, and we moved more by
sparse starlight, the bounty of $100,000 on his brow now widely known.
The day he heard of Lincoln's expiration I was beside him, and he stared

ahead and whispered, "The fools, they have undone us." At that moment he looked more Quixote than Lion Heart, and I knew he was thinking even a tyrant was preferable to chaos and anarchy. "They will bear down upon us," he added, "with zeal," and turned again to his thoughts.

Jim caught up later and leaned his head on my shoulder. "You wanted to be a soldier, Rowley. These are the times that define us." His drawl was always a comfort, but I saw in his eyes an awareness that even the false feast was ending. He promised to rub liniment into the arm I'd strained helping him rewheel a wagon. All in all, it was a day of trials.

The heavens were, as I said, cascading by midnight, and the chief had gone ahead, but Miss Varina's group reined in at the hamlet of Abbeville, and next day we limped on to Irwinville and halted by a stream. I could not say aught of the site, for the falling rain kept us blind. To dally seemed unsafe, and it was hard labor to sustain even a simmer fire for coffee. Horses snorted, the smoke from their nostrils an omen.

Every one of us was tensed, for reports placed plunderers on our flanks, stragglers from Sherman sporting nooses and leaderless outliers with a nose for gold. Yet we rested. I napped early after spending my last candle helping Jim sew frogs on Jeff's favorite gown. He had but three left, the others abandoned of necessity. They had become our only armor, the souvenirs of halcyon hours in Richmond, but those times seemed less memory than dream. He kneaded my neck and back muscles with herb paste till they relaxed enough for me to slip into Morpheus' arms.

Not long after, I woke to find Jim gone and quickly joined my watch on the perimeter. Through the drumming of deluge I could soon hear horses at a gallop and voices. I spurred to pass the alarm. This was our worst fear— our party at ease and sleepy, them eager for booty and reward. Unhappily, my mount went down in a rillet. Pure confusion, and all around me the fighting commenced—chaos in darkness, disembodied sounds, orders shouted, the rattle of tack, hammers cocking and the cold rasp of blades unsheathed. Random discharge of weapons. I found myself scrambling on all fours, stunned but uninjured. Not even the trees were visible. The way was lost.

Ahead, in obscured darkness with only a knife edge of dawn to aid, I made out a dark figure bearing down with a guidon lance, and when I reached for my revolver, it was missing in the dark. I fumbled in the mud with desperation and no success. You would not be in this coach now, son, your father would never have come calf-squalling into this world, if another horseman had not interposed, and it was dear Jim Speed, ever the guardian, sword drawn, body locked and leaning in the saddle like a jouster, but the flagged lance had the longer reach, and Jim took it full in the belly before he was able to raise and hack. Yet hack he did, and both riders went down shouting.

I could hear more gear clattering and crash of hooves in the filling ruts as I scrambled to where Jim was sprawled, but when I reached his side, his eyes were frozen open, their pools veiling in the morning light. I am not ashamed to say my tears showered as the fallen Yankee's voice also ceased beneath my hand.

This was why I returned on foot to Jeff's tent in time to witness the moment of capture. Most firing in the confusion turned out to be two Federal regiments acting independently—the 4th Michigan and 1st Wisconsin, as it happens—assailing one another in the Georgia dark with small arms and not certain whom they had surprised. This, it seems, bears the stamp of justice.

Back at camp, the First Lady had sent her maid out with a bucket to accompany the President and make him seem another servant girl while he sought his horse, but he would have none of it and approached the man shouting for him to halt. I am told Jeff addressed the trooper in Chippewa—he was fluent—as he ripped away his skirts and assumed a belligerent stance.

What had we hoped? To rendezvous with the ship *Shenandoah* and make our way back to the land whose señoritas had shown Jeff the art of a haughty flounce and how to drape a mantilla. Fiesta, new recruits, hope and revenge. Instead, he got cold bonds chafing, Macon and Augusta by rail, on to Savannah and the steamer *William P. Clyde* to their capital, which was festooned in crepe for mourning. Under guard and in double chains, but note this: He and Varina at least were granted the privacy of their tent for moments before the provost took him out and applied the shackles. He pled his wet state and begged opportunity to change. In that rare kindness, the captors allowed him to quell the worst stirrings of suspicion. He stripped away his distaff finery and emerged in a gray suit and vest, an unbroken man, even to the superficial eye of common soldiers. For years he was thus, all dignity and restraint, a veritable sphinx. What he said when they clasped the wrist cuffs was, "God's will be done." Gethsemane, you remember.

The Frenchman Diderot wrote, as you know, that the word is certainly not the thing so much as the flash of light that presents the thing to our eyes. I offer these words in that spirit and supplement witness with speculation. "Why?" you are asking, "Why did a war hero, a Kentucky planter and diplomat, the master of Brierfield in Dixie's deep heart, find himself drawn to kohl, rouge and swishing skirts of crimson cambric? Why that path to the eccentric? You will have heard that the mountebank Barnum charged admission to view the very petticoats he claimed Davis wore, along with the jerkylike mummy of J. W. Booth, but the display was lost when the circus burned. A hoax, anyway, but I know this much. Jeff had often voiced his love for thespian lore, especially the sorrows and delights of Shakespeare. Juliet, Desdemona, Calpurnia and bloody Mrs. Macbeth—he could say so many speeches with a voice at once eloquent and choking. The roles, in their own time, were always acted by boys.

Distress no doubt played its appointed role. He was elected by a handful of aristocrats and served as provisional president for a year until his office was decreed official. He never enjoyed the lever of a popular vote or any other sort but what the self-appointed firebrands ordained. This was no source of confidence, and the times required a mandate.

I recall one morning months before the capture, soon after the Brown's Island explosion had killed sixty-two women workers. He had been to the site and spoken as nurse and solace, soothing the wounded, comforting the kin. "I suffer for them, Rowley," he said, "though they are truly the stronger sex." That night, he returned to the island escorted only by the serving boy Jim Limber and clad in a maidservant's homespun, his face shrouded by a mourning matron's veil. For hours he fed them soup hauled down from his kitchen. Back in his chamber at dawn, he woke me for company and said, "Perhaps by stealth I can better justify the station I am doomed to occupy."

And when he stilled the surging crowds at the bread riot, he again mentioned needing the strength of women. If I understand correctly, he was far ahead of his time, a man eager to contain both genders, aiming at completeness, and the next evening in private, he commented on my ebony *sous-jupe* by saying I had the eye of a seamstress. That, as time proved, was prophecy.

And yet Jeff held hard devices as well and believed slavery a divine decree to protect the minstrel mind and those he deemed lazy heathens. Some notions he was yoked with for life. He could praise God in one clause and finish the sentence with a flourish about Africans being a mistake of creation. And though he could always muster the tone of *noblesse oblige,* when he raised his pealing baritone on "The Harp That Once in Tara's Hall," it was pure artillery, the sentiment of pearl and velvet set on a backdrop of lead. The world is a mystery I do not pretend to understand.

He was unique, yet even the unhistoried have known of Beauty Stuart and Yellow Tavern, the Gettysburg folly. That swashbuckling idiot. Is it not obvious that he, too, dressed over the line, was a man with the heart of an Amazon, especially when charging a target? Not to mention Pickett. You've seen the pictures, his oiled ringlets and peahen posture. He tossed his glossy hair like Danton and curled his handlebar. That posh man was peevish as Jeff, though he lacked the aura of greatness. Oh, he was one of us, I warrant, but he feared his urges and chose to act the paladin with a bully's swagger, to strut the Italian and deny as he asked his boys to wade into blood for him. And they complied, but who knows if he wore pantaloons with his staff or fondled bombazine with eager fingers? I have seen his merry eye smile over a captured wagon of Union officers' tunics. In short, what matter? Battle is the soldier's test and talent, decisiveness, charisma and wisdom the only questions when you judge a commander. Those years under siege, resources frail or none or few, and yet Jefferson Davis kept us to the task, our hope before us. A hurricane in his anger, a mother in forgiveness, he drew strength and vigor from our discipline of masquerade when shells fell into cowering Richmond like the shouts of an angry Lord.

And afterward? I took the new oath of allegiance and accepted pardon. We all signed parole and dispersed, some to Texas, Mexico or the jungles of Cuba. I sold the horse and McClellan saddle, then turned north to my own home country and turned my angry energy to commerce. The nightmare of Reconstruction dragged by like a sledge, but I prospered and earned the price of an education, matriculated, then took my eye for haberdashery to Savannah. No more cunning and guns, just concentration. I specialized in quality broadcloth and saw fresh ways to shape a wing and collar, always wondering what Jim would think, or Jeff himself, of my drawings and the final designs. Fad and fashion, I led instead of followed, imagining black pekin strips of gauze and moiré over yellow taffeta.

Soon your grandmother appeared, herself a vision, and we changed the look of women, pioneering the slip, the yoke, wool twills. Aberrations like lamé silk harem pants and the lampshade tunic made me laugh, but I relied on taste and tact to shape the market. The rest is sheer luck and economics.

Jim himself was never angry, though he had seen too much to be soft. It was woodsmoke he smelled of, and fresh bread, with something else— wild berry? ginger? The sound of him was a razor scraping as he looked into the blade of a Bowie. Who could forget him spinning the star wheels of his spurs or emitting a low whistle when impressed. He relished stroking the white blaze of his horse's muzzle and possessed the loveliest untamed tenor, be it hymn or ballad, come-all-ye or courting carol.

That is why we make this journey, to honor him where his stone steadfasts in Chattanooga. Not his body, of course, which Yankees no doubt rolled into some pauper's pit in Macon at the swamp end of Rose Hill. They have a small river there, but nothing like the one he floated on, wary of rapids, knowing the bends even by starlight, steering his crew wide of the fuel-stop groggeries and grab-alls, the pirate holts and blowdowns where moccasins nested in a writhe knot. He could thread a needle by the light of a goldfinch at midnight. He could soothe wounds and call country doves out of their thickets, but he could shoot like a Boone and lift a grown man over his head. Deep eyes like a doe, a taste for ant-tiny whips of lace, a voice like wing-cooled honey, a mind for details like a quartermaster, and yet the heart of a panther. He was all a man should be, and I never told him, to my shame. A rare breed, boy. The world will not see his kind again.

Even now, though, seeing your tunic's buttons, I think of the waste and carnage, all the slaughter I saw, the sorrow, and here at the end? The steady thunder of a train in a tunnel, a man's life fading. Touch the buttons that keep your gabardine closed. Do you know what they are, those rough white half-moons? They're bone, boy, and don't ever forget such details by which we're measured.

This will likely be my last journey. Now here's a flask and silver cup, as we cross the ridge and descend the mountain. It would please me no end if you would join me in a toast. "A dram to gallant Jim and Jeff himself, together the pride and prize of the Confederacy and my heart."

I complied and drank deep, as darkness like pleated velvet smothered all but the southbound cadence of the train.

Uke Rivers Delivers

The week after my daddy sowed me in the marriage furrow, Mama and Selena went arrowheading over at Ocmulgee, walking from the river to the earth mounds the rattlesnake Creeks raised to bury their kings and have church, and Mama claimed the Indian spirits from the ground must of smoked up and threw a birth curse while her and Selena was scratching out flints, which was all supposed to explain why I come out of the oven fully-haired and rusty-looking, yodeling and not more-sized than a bun. My daddy Strother didn't credit it, though, and he beat Mama near to death, saying nothing that piddling could be his get, allowing as how I maybe wasn't even human and should not be let to live. Miz Revis across the road called up Sheriff Ruffton, and he got there on time to haul Daddy off before Mama was all the way dead, but Daddy never showed his whiskers in Macon after that. I don't know what become of him, and I have had to manage without a guiding man figure in my life. For a small-built person such as myself, that makes it all worse, though for a spell (as you know) I was getting by and actually starting to prosper.

Mama loved me like a regular baby, never mind my puniness, and she called me "Pet," though my Christian name was Parham; Parham Rivers I was, but you know I changed my name to Uke long before I ever cut an album, and people did say it was witchwork, how such a little bitty body could be attached to fingers so quick and clever. Some folks said I was a midget, a pygmy, a dwarf, and ought to be sent straight to the carnival, but Doc Bowles, he said, Nossir, I was just little. At first he figured it was just a stage I'd ride over and get my growth. Didn't transpire. Doctors don't know pig shit from sorghum.

They was always losing me, Mama and Selena and Jonette, and once when I fell asleep in the butter churn, I woke up to find them all aweep and turning the house upside-under. The worst thing that almost tragedied out was when Roy Barrett, Daddy's favorite coon hound, run off with me in his mouth and tried to bury me in the pine woods. Lucky for me it had been a dry summer, and the red clay wasn't no picnic to tear into, so Selena found us and whipped him with the hoe stick while Mama gave me the rescue. I still bear the marks.

Some people believed I was special blessed and wanted me to touch their babies or their sucking calves once I got to walking myself and talking like somebody with the tongues. I wasn't no other help around the house but wiping dishes, shelling peas or silking corn, which I learned early, and I was a pure-T hardship, since Mama had to hand-sew all my britches, coveralls and shirts. Shoes was always a problem, and I was afflicted with surprising proportion, organized like a tiny man already and not much baby chubbiness. Other details I won't go into, but youngster clothes wasn't much use. The family still loved me, though; I guess it was my kitteny disposition and belting out songs from Sunday school all the time. I kept Jesus on my lips and in the house. That was my donation to life.

To make me feel more like I belonged, Uncle Laster drove me down to LaGrange to see the midget rasslers. Sky Low Low, Pancho the Bull, Bashful and Mohawk Manny were the openers on the tag-team card, but seeing them trounce and gouge and beller didn't make me a better fit in the world. Afterwards, I hummed harmony to the radio a while, then pretended to sleep the rest of the way home. I didn't want to talk about the flinging and cavorting spectacle of those pint-sized naked specimens, but I made my manners when he dropped me off, lots of "I 'preciate" and "Thank you kindly," though it didn't set well with me. Freaks is what they was, and I saw no kinship comfort in all their monkeyshining.

At preaching, Brother Duke Altross would say a special Samaritan prayer for me, and I sat up front so wouldn't no heads block my view. Once a rooster come after me in the churchyard and Blister Ferrum had to grab me up, thinking I was about to be pecked to death right there on God's holy ground. I had turned to face the bird, though, and was about to sing him under, though I don't remember how I knew. Something just seized me.

I know I'm being slow now to get this out, but the why of it all don't allow for shortcuts. I was right quick at books but didn't much fancy school, where they snickered and tittered at me. I was a mite scared, too. Chaps can be cruel, and I had to hear "freak" and "pipsqueak" more times than roasting ears has kernels. I couldn't hardly tote a satchel, and the teachers was mortified somebody'd damage or misplace me. First graders was always promising to shut me in a locker. Once they tried to tackle and strip me to see did I have a tail.

What I did learn there from Miz Isley was that I had the perfect pitch and could tune a piano in a Mississippi minute. That was when Mama sent off to Sears for the kiddie fiddle and I learned to stroke it. "Wildwood Flower" was my favorite right off—I'd heard them spooky Carters on the radio—but I learned "Blessed Assurance" and all the holy ones along with the barn-dance tunes, and when I was old enough I played a bit at night church and hayrides and such, till it came clear to some folks my gift was a little twisted.

That made getting day work hard, though, because one time I was playing "Abide with Me" for prayer meeting, and I felt myself slipping too deep into the music, like the strings was more important than the worship feel, like they had their own plan I was being pulled into. The notes come up around me like a caul, and I couldn't see clearly. The whole world was a red sound. Then everybody in the pews commenced to shiver and weep, and when I hit the last chorus, I swear to you the overhead lights was blinking and flickering in time with my strings. It was awful, and afterwards, not many folks came up to thank me. Even the preacher give me the softest handshake on record and turned quick to comfort some other sinner. After that, most of the congregation held their distance. I kept to myself and played for the hogs and birds and squirrels, who have their own connection to Jesus. Everything with ears is burning for the Word.

At last I got 'prenticed out to Even Whitlaw, the pest killer, who was not churchy and needed a spry helper to go after infesters. I could crawl through folks' attics and under the floor with traps or poison and the long pincer stick for hauling out the dead. I took the Daisy air rifle after fairydiddles nesting under the rafters and learned to figure my money like a storekeeper, which has come in handy. Got so I wasn't spooked by your snake nor your rat nor any other vermin, and people snickering didn't hurt the way it used to. I began to believe Mama might be right to say I was charmed. My hair went white as the hot tip of a fire poker and my eyes got bluer. I started to sprout chin whiskers. All in all, I was getting normal, except for girls and my size: I quit rising at three-feet-six, not much taller than a goat.

By sixteen years I knowed the fiddle wasn't all that suited for my hands, and it hurt my neck to chin-grip it and twist my left arm about like willow driftwood. Besides, it was a child's model I was sawing. The notes was thin, half whispery, and that just didn't set right. The music wanted to be full-size. That's when I seen him on Myrna's Philco—Arthur Godfrey—and he had that ukulele twinging out music that hit my ears just apple-pie perfect. He looked like a Holiness preacher that we'd see waving his Testament on market morning under the cracked Confederate statue on the square, but his vocal chords had this soothy tone, all milk and sourwood honey, and some voice inside my head whispered, "You can sing like that."

I had saved out a heap of varmint money, so I got Stella Bresh, the pretty mail lady, to post an order to Monkey Ward, who sent me back my first five-string tenor uke, which the Martin factory in Nazareth, Pennsylvania, was making for the catalog people. It was mostly curly koa from Hawaii with rosewood binding, but the best feature was it sported pearl-mother inlays of snowflake on the fingerboard, and they always felt so cool to the touch, I knew I'd done found a home. You likely know Ukulele Ike had awoke the luthiers that there was money in them things, and near about anybody could play them. Pretty soon *Pinocchio* would come along with "When You Wish upon a Star," and that would crank up a bona fide craze. For good luck I did finally learn "Pua Tubarose," which I gave a bluegrass spin, despite it being in Ike's honor, but mostly I didn't stick to the hula stuff. My voice had a good quaver, and I could be mournful like the whip-poor-wills those Ocmulgee Creeks prayed to and carved into their tobacco pipes. Sometimes a notion would take me over, and I could put the joy in sorrow, even if it gave me the willies those first few times. I was just happy to feel myself drawed into something working on a grand scale, even something dark.

It was Stella herself that eventually took over from Selena to keep me fed and safe and in clothes. I know people will talk and say it's creepy, me being married to a normal-sized woman, but Stella had drove the mail to our house for years and we always talked, mostly about bagworms or swine fever or the crop weather. Then when she brung that uke, she said, "I want to hear this thing when you've got it working." She was a soft gal with strawberry-blond curls and a great old smile, and I was already mooning after her like the bear after the picnic basket. I mean, I went at that uke stick like a firecat, repeating every exercise in the little book. This was before Jumpin' Jimmy's teaching series, so I had to fill in a lot myself, but I had the knack, getting good licks right away, learning all the chords, refining, fickling with my fingernails and doubling the strum. In two weeks I did "Toot Toot Tootsie" in G at the mailbox, and the song was singing me so entirely, she was nearly 'bout won over. The rest of our courting was porch-swinging and talking, or her just sipping tea while I showed off. We'd go to a diner or church, and I didn't give hoot nor holler what those crackers whispered.

Stella was the one that taught me tippling, and she'd drive me over the river to the Hollow Log Lounge to play for the dancers, who gave me quarters and dollars. Sometimes when I'd get a little sipping whisky in my system, I'd get on the bar and pose like the stuffed bear cub they have on a shelf. I wasn't much bigger. Them people laughed *with* me, and they knew I was wicked on the strings, so they 'preciated. I'd got my hands on a book called *Nice Songs for Naughty People,* so I kept them laughing and dancing. Them cotton mill folks took me for myself. They took my heart's measure and didn't show a mean bone. That's what being a show can do for you, if you handle it proper, even if something you can't name might be in control.

Likely everybody knows that "ukulele" means "jumping flea," which is what the dark natives on Hawaii said when they saw them Portuguese sailors strumming on the *machete de braga,* which was what they called their wee-tiny guitars. Some say "uke" means an old word for "gift" in luau land, but anybody can see how nimble you've got to stitch and flick it, like a flea flock trying to dance on a hot skillet. Some will opt out for the mandolin or lute and say how they're more tricky and able for cleaner frenzy, but my fingers is too frailish to get intricate on the mando's double strings, and they will cut you. The ukes, though, I've got a wall of 'em from the Gibson concert and two Martin M's to the Kamaka pineapple and Washburn Taro Patch with herringbone purfling. The soundboards all have a sweet sheen, and the strings is mostly nylon or gut, so they won't take a mind to bite, which is not to say such picking the way I do is without a cost or easy.

When Stella took the Asian, I couldn't much help her. The doctor come in and give her pills and tonics and even shots, but it was no use. I played her favorites softly at her bedside till my fingers bled. No use. She burned till she went blue cold. Why I didn't get flu myself is a mystery, but I never took sick from it, and we put her in the ground with lots of yellow flowers. I was planning to plonk and sing "Amazing Grace," but when I saw the clouds brewing, I played "Raindrops Keep Falling" in a dark way nobody had ever heard before, and the sky broke and downpoured till they had to carry me back to the undertaker's truck. You see, I thought something in my music could reach out into the other place and call her back, but it turned out not so. I was shook up after that and wouldn't hardly leave the house. Mama and them come over and read me scripture and cooked and all, but I wanted to be dead myself. The uke just picked up dust and the strings soured, but one day my eyes fell on the inlay, and the snowflakes seemed to promise life would get better. I knew I'd never get over losing Stell, but you have to look ahead, and I know a body might expect me to say something here about missing the sex part of our love, and how it was. Anybody'd be curious, but I won't talk about that. Some secrets are secret.

When the first album come out—*Uke Rivers Delivers*—I was famous pretty quick. My note-work had took on a sassy tone nobody else could manage, and my voice still had the hint of something through a vestry keyhole, but it was world-wearied and sad, too, with a taint of the Indian, a hint of the snake. First fairs and festivals and radio from Valdosta to Nashville, with lots of prizes coming my way and so much applause that a fly wouldn't have a Chinaman's chance of survival in a room where I was playing. Then I went to the big TV Sullivan, who talked to me like a knee baby. You know he had that Mexican mouse puppet and wanted me to sing with it. "Bullshit," I told them. I slashed out a Johnny Rivers kind of treatment on "Somewhere over the Rainbow," tossing about my icy hair and reeling out the full amazing range of my tiny voice for the first time in public, and after that, I never again needed to be caresome about money, despite having to order many of my personal goods made special. People wanted Uke everywhere, and my red western-style suits with the cuff braid and my derby hat are famous now. A tailor will even come to my house to measure for them, but it's not just the garments, you know: even my razors, my chairs, watch, cups and stuff. I've seen Paris, though, and the queen of London. A music man is a traveling man.

After the second album went gold was when I moved up to Atlanta and had a regular saloon gig at Emry's Picks and Strings. The big-city country-western crowd adored what I could muster to be rowdy around, but I kept Jesus in my program for Mama and Selena, who would ride the rails on the Nancy Hanks Local from Macon till Mama took a bad turn from the heart trouble. What made me a star, I expect, was my own songs like "The Lonesome Snowflake," "White Crow" and "Cropper's Sorrow" and the spicy string-ring I could conjure for the more mellow stuff. One Christmas Eve when I was singing the mournful ballad of the church fiddler, which I tagged "Shiver and Weep," all the clocks stopped. Some people's watches, too, dead-still. It was like the *Twilight Zone* stories on the TV. Some folks hung around and couldn't stop jabbering about it, but a fair few slipped away quiet, looking at me over the shoulder. Shoot, it made the papers, and nobody could give it sense. Yeah, that sort of stuff is good for publicity, but I can't let it worry me. When that wind from another world takes you by the scruff and shakes you, you got to decide. I always wanted the ride, even if I couldn't reckon the cost. Even if things went a little blurry and left me short-breathed after a wild tune, I was willing.

To get by, in the practical way of speaking, I lived with a man helper who could cook and drive and liked to speak to people on the telephone, but life was still pretty low for me, since Stella went, and I kept thinking about how a man needs a woman, body needs a body, skin wants skin. Size don't change that.

The next winter I met Sunny, who you know became the problem, but I couldn't of been happier at the start. When I clapped eyes on her, she was floating across the barroom in a cloud of cigarette smoke, everybody else foggy, but her features clear and shining like something in art. She was copper-headed with pink skin, though her considerable head and stubby limbs made her slightly ungraceful. She appeared to be shook up by my playing from the get-go and started showing up at Picks and Strings on Saturdays about ten, sitting up front on a whirly stool, smoking Herbert Tarreytons and requesting "Ain't She Sweet" every time. I was happy as a toad in clover to see a small woman with a social side and not cutting the fool at some circus. The first time we had a parley, I learned she was a sure-fire midget and had two others in her family. It didn't hold her back none, though. She was smart as a whip, working at Georgia Baptist Hospital with the X-rays, and she rode the bus and bought groceries and all that, had Hank Williams records and a teakettle collection and neighbor friends she shopped and played cards with. She drank those Bloody Marys, and I'd send her one from the bar. Pretty soon we was going other places together, but she was from over in Tennessee, and I couldn't be sure she had fleshly urges or that I could suit them, so I held my horses and chewed my lip. Court and spark: I knew the time would come.

When it did, on her pink sofa, I should of knowed her bashful ways was too quirky to be honest. First time I tried to kiss her, she backed off and started talking fast about how ladies need insurance. She kept sipping her tomato juice drink, fanning herself with a magazine and saying "Fools rush in" and she wasn't no fool. I couldn't figure it out, till she said love should go to marriage or be smothered. I hadn't plotted it out that way, but I didn't have no immediate objection. She batted her eyes, and when I started nodding and smiling in agreement, things went swiftly to the private act. I will say this, she had the fullest, sweetest lips you could imagine, and her hospital costume in the bedroom was a special treat.

So I fell for it, and we started planning, getting a few folks lined up, including Emry and his wife and my two sisters, though it was sad Mama couldn't make the trip. Three weeks later, we hitched in what is called a "private ceremony." I played "Oh, Promise Me" and threw in a lot of technical fancywork and vibrato. It wasn't like times when the music's claw reached out and shook me, but it was good enough. The flowers were white, the bride wore blue velvet, and I was decked out in my best scarlet suit and dapper chapeau. The judge himself snapped the pictures. Everybody shuffled and flat-footed when I ended the ceremony with a take on "Cherokee Rose" that surprised even me and popped open all the champagne.

Sunny quit her job at the hospital lickety-split, which didn't trouble me at all, and rode the train with me or the car with Danny, my manager-driver, who had always been a pearl of a fellow. He was a quiet sort and kindly enough that you wouldn't know he was normal sized.

You wouldn't know he had the women itch, either, not in all the time he worked for me. But Sunny seemed to make him blush and stutter at first; then they got comfortable and chummy and said things in a low voice when I was tuning up or taking sound checks. They seemed to get serious about their drinking, dropping the cocktails for Rebel Yell in a bottle, and they'd give each other the giggles like teen children, and pretty soon, they'd started to slip out during one of my sets. "Smoking," they said, but they'd be gone an hour. It's a habit I never took up myself, tobacco, and I'd never known Danny to do that before, either, and though it's a fact that I'm bantam-puny and not strong as your average man, I'm still not stupid.

The two of them seemed to have secret codes, because I'd see a high-sign wink or rolled eyes when they were talking in front of me, and before long, Sunny sort of turned from me. I mean, she'd shrug off my arm and say in that Olive Oyl voice of hers, "Oughtn't you go practice, darling," like I was some ten-thumbs beginner. She took to pouting and keeping long silence, coming lively again only when we went out for a performance or some party. It was a strange turn in her nature, and I was worried it might be all those years around the X-rays. And Danny, well, he became a closer part of our lives than I ever had in mind. It was about that time that Mama died, and I was too shook up to render her favorites at the wake. They just played the tape, and I took to my bed for a week with nerve pills and Wild Turkey.

Last Wednesday night I got wore out from putting in shelves to hold my awards and trophies, which had overflowed from the mantel a good piece back. The power drill is a heavy tool for me, and I don't care to risk my wrists by overtaxing. When I offered to take Sunny to a Gregory Peck picture show, she allowed as how she'd as soon stay home, curl up on the couch with Lucy and Desi and Little Ricky. She had a pitcher of tomato drinks and sat there in the fur wrap I had give her for her birthday. It was two foxes all soft and rusty biting one another, but dead, staring glass-eyed at the world, and Sunny give me a kind of dirty sneer and brushed in my direction with her limp hand. "Go find an elf party, Jukebox," she said, and right then I was sure it was time to sort it all out, to just walk around and add things up and ponder. I was in a state, I'll tell you, feeling jealous and like I was being robbed of my rewards in life. I knowed Sunny wasn't no Stella, couldn't even come close, but I still calculated respect wasn't too much to ask, even from a mini-bitch, even from a drunk.

A thin rain was falling, making the streets shine with oily light and the neon store signs all distorted and saying nothing. Cars would rush past with a whoosh, and as I walked down Ponce de Leon, I saw the flowers knocked down from the dogwoods by the wind that was prowling around the corners and swooping up here and there. The petals in the air made me think of the uke's pearly snowflakes my fingers hardly noticed anymore as I squeezed the chords and slid along the tight wires, and the sound of all that water made it seem more like a river than a city.

I knew I'd made a mistake this time, since nobody could have the soothing voice and healing touch of Stella. I thought back to those evenings when she'd come in from her route and take a showerbath to get the road dust off her, and we'd sit in the parlor, her blowing simple harmony on the French harp, me plucking and strumming "Buffalo Gals," "Bluesette," "Arkansas Traveler," "Delia's Gone" and so on. She'd stroke my arm and call me "Par," which was her shortcut for my real self, "Parham." It was peaceful and lightsome and sweet, her eyes bright as a new thimble. As I always say, she was an angel. Thinking that made my breath run short, and my fingers began to get the tingling to try some new chord changes I wanted to work into "Midnight Special," so I whipped around and headed back to the apartment. Besides, I was wet as a stormed-on dog.

It's for true I came in quiet, not rattling the keys nor turning on a light. Not sneaking, I was just distracted, caught up, making straight for the Godfrey Vega DeLuxe behind the sofa. I wasn't even thinking what I'd earlier been mulling. I didn't plan no misbehavior, because Mama Rivers always said you got to move on, and something was making my fingers burn to pick them strings. But then I caught the sound of a tussling from the bedroom, and through the door I saw weird figures in the haze of streetlights sliced sharp by the open blinds. Then I could make out Sunny's little body jumping about, the foxes on her neck flailing. Danny's voice in the shadows said, "Oh, my baby, oh," as the mattress spronged, and I could hear the strings snapping deep in my heart. I reckon my daddy's devil side come out in me at last or that old voice that whispered in me but wasn't mine. Arrowheads, whip-poor-wills, Ocmulgee drums—I don't know. I didn't even wait to ploy it out. The power drill was still there: a Craftsman, plugged in to the extension. Something seized me, like when I'm deep into a tune. I whipped it up, hopped onto the bed, pushed the bit to his head and gripped the trigger before the trysters knowed enough to give up moaning for screaming. It was just seconds, the drill whining toward high C, and then the lower drone pitch like after you get through a plank. I'd heard something close to that music before, but what my heart was feeling I didn't recognize at all. I didn't even seem like me. After the fit passed, I just remember a dark spray like a fountain, then the troopers and sirens and red lights flashing around the room. They locked my hands up behind my back with the police bracelets, and somebody said, "Son, you're completely arrested. You have the right to be silent."

My fingers get all fidgety and stiff and cold when I can't strum and fret my way to ease. Too long without playing and I get the chills and fevers. Mama always said, "Idle hands, idle hands." I'm just glad she's not around to see how a saving skill might veer wrong and how her boy who just wanted to please has been led to suffer and misbehave.

I reckon that's all you need to know. It could be the Creek village sachem's curse coming back on me or maybe my daddy's crazy ways, but I don't figure how the judge can hold me answerable for something that hexy and deep-sourced in the family blood, beyond my doing. Uncontrollable forces are working hard inside us all. I was seized and changed and didn't have a thought to damage a soul. Everything was whirl and blur. Looking back, though, I swear it felt like music.

Bitterwolf

The ones he caught he led back to the soldiers in shackles—one, a pair, occasionally a coffle of a dozen. They rattled in their irons along the deer paths and over the ridges of Nantahala. They skirted bedrock outcrops and trod along deadfalls. They stumbled near Junaluska or rested Where the Bears Held Council. In rain or roasting sun the captives shuffled across swales and often fell on the steep declines. They wept and begged and cursed. Sometimes in the instant before surrender, they sang.

Others, however, he killed as they fled. The Deer Clan, the Twister Clan, Paint, Wild Potato, Blue. He called out in warning, and if they did not stop, he lifted the Hall's carbine from his pommel or drew the Colt. He shot them as they broke cover from a laurel hell or splashed down a streambed, disturbing the tarnished trout he had been partial to since boyhood. He aimed for the spine, between the shoulders, where Heron Woman had promised the Stayers would grow wings if the white men pursued them. No feathers sprouted. They did not fly. Their hunter was not a white man.

The ones he captured were locked in cells and rationed bad bread, corn grits and stagnant water, while he devoured venison, kale and sweet potatoes with flat tavern ale. Their chains were looped through heavy rings in the floor, the straw filthy with waste, their only window a spyhole so high they could see a mere circle of heaven. They were cramped and without a fire. Though he did not know from observation that they were taunted and spat upon by the white guards, he must have suspected it. Though he heard them calling out, asking for scraps or mercy, he chose never to speak or turn. He would not see into their eyes nor hear their songs.

Those who survived until their number approached three score were transported, walking down to the station, then in fetid wagons, on muleback, shanks' mare, tumbrel and caisson, always bound, always under the eye of a rifle, westward, westward, the lash tearing their clothing and flesh, bracelets chafing, road fever rampant, until the wraiths they had become, those who were able to rise when they fell, reached the Oklahoma Territory where their people were living on arid land beside a creek the government agent called a river. There, on the new reservation, they yearned for the sight of familiar knob, bluff and knuckle, the black haw, chestnut oak and flowering ash, the expanse of Shaconage, their High Country of Great Smoke. As they learned break-back hoe farming and how easily an acre could eat a family, they continued to curse their captor, and the song they sang was a plea to the blood god for his death.

The time he found John Blackfox creeling fish from his willow trap the two locked eyes for an instant, knowing they had met as boys while gathering firewood. John Blackfox was of the Paint Clan, and he had taken to the fir woods with his brother Lewis, dodging the rattle of soldiers' tack and the smell of their mules, their clay pipes and trash pits. The hunter surprised the Blackfoxes before they could break camp that morning, but he did not see Lewis lying on the sleeping platform high in a hemlock.

"You are the twisted heart," John Blackfox had called out, reaching for his old British rifle. "You are the bane of your people. You wear the white man's shame with his clothing. I will send you to the Gate of Darkness for the sake of the people."

But Blackfox was lame from running too hard, and his spirit was lame also, weary with weeks of restless sleep and meager meals always eaten on the move.

"Do not force me to kill you, Paint Clan. The bullet is faster than your thinking. I wish only to deliver you, but if your hand touches the weapon, I will strike, though your blood will give me no pleasure."

Lewis was but a boy and had no weapon. Later, when he was captured and taken west, he told the wraiths in their chains that he saw the eyes of a panther blazing from the hunter's face, and the dark red horse was breathing smoke, the sky spinning.

The report from the hunter's gun sent redbirds flying up like a blood spray, and John Blackfox fell backwards into the water with a new eye in his brow looking for the sun. The boy told anyone who would listen that the hunter growled as he dismounted, and he feared seeing his brother eaten, so he drew back from the edge of the branches.

"I heard him sing a song from the other world," the boy told anyone in flat Oklahoma who would listen. "It was not a man's song, and I feared he would find my perch and eat me as well, but he was soon gone, like a beast who has eaten his fill, and my brother lay in the stream, his life spoiling the water, turning it red. His hands were missing, and the sky was the color of stones scorched in a fire ring. I wet myself and then I was weeping. Why did he have no hands?"

This was early in the searching, and word traveled quickly among the scattered bands that a demon had been spawned from their own kind. Few were aware of his history, but they believed he had powers and a thirst for blood of his kindred. And he would steal the hands of the dead.

Years before, when he skulked about the village as a boy, it had been called Oconaluftee, which meant place of the strange speakers, but now the pale people who brought skins of deer and fox and otter to the new trading post called it Kituwah or Cherokee, after those who drank in sips and who had been marched off en masse and those others still, nearly a year later, hiding in the forest, keeping a cold camp, refusing removal, uprooting almost every morning and burying their tracks, waste pits, scraps of their game, their ceremonial stones. The *ulatidi,* the fugitives, did not risk the noise of a shot, even if they still had powder for their old fusils, and relied on slingstone, snare and arrow. They swam through the shadows, deeper and deeper into the dark precincts of the Nantahala which he knew and loved from youthful solitude, a demesne he himself could not bear to abandon. They fled and concealed themselves in hope of staying near their spirit places, the sacred plots where their ancestors had been laid, the wind-swayed hemlocks and plants like cohosh and ripweed that healed their ailments, sharpened their senses and brought their gods closer. Trespassers in their own homelands, they beseeched Ancient Red and the First Hunter, but their words went unanswered. *Adanvo,* their spirits, could never be at ease.

He no longer thought of them as kin. His father, Elijah Not-Ross, had been cast out for marrying the Shawnee thief's widow against the orders of the elders, had been forced to fashion his cabin on the edge of the village, to scorch and adze his canoes from tree trunks in isolation. He farmed his corn and cane and a patch of cotton alone, for he was sentenced to the silence and not allowed to meet their eyes. Elijah Not-Ross was not permitted to worship with the others, denied the fire ring and sourwood rods, the Booger Dance with its healing masks, as well as the new communion, and with the woman he began to invent his own practices with the flowers that glow in darkness and the bark of the willow, the pelt of the fallow deer. They spoke to Skunk and Raven and asked the snakes to come back biting their neighbors. Elijah was clothed in sorrow. Even with the buffalo long gone, and life becoming smaller as their young men went deeper into the mountains, the tribe would not accept him back to the center. He worked until his hands became stiff and his skin a coarse, unchewed leather. His face could not smile, and the clans began to call him a Bitterwolf, which meant he was under the spell of the Shawnee woman, and his ghost would walk forever without the pipe of peace.

His son, also, abandoned hope of belonging, of sharing his wanderings in the forest, of hearing the tribal stories and shouting with joy in the ball game under the watch of a village girl. He could listen to their flutes in the firefly evenings and learned the old stories from any chants they did not hold to a whisper, but he was shunned by daylight and given the gesture for a pariah. He grew bitter, also a wolf, *wayah,* though he too was birth-named Elijah by the mission. His father taught him the bow, the blowgun and snare, the keen edge, sounding the trees and felling them, snaking the logs downslope to the rapids. He tanned skins with a brain scrape fashioned from the butt plate of a musket and followed his father's path, learning every ridge and rut, teaching the trees to lean and then fall gently and later to yearn for floating on water. In the regional schoolhouse he sat apart and kept his face turned to the hornbook. He walked the valleys and crests, dug roots in the forest and learned the ways of panther, wolf, opossum and bear. Once, walking the hackles of a bald with his father at the close of a cold day, he pointed to the sky. Two hawks collided to cling and spiral from sight beyond the treeline. Their sharp cries carved a mighty song, but his father said it is called love-of-the-other-self and not to be trusted. With no one to confide in, he saved his longings to tell the fire at evening. His secrets were hidden by the sinew thread he sewed with, cached in the hollows a hammerbird had opened in dead trees. He had no discourse with the people, but from cover he watched the village boys playing hoop games with an envy that sharpened to scorn.

He could remember, the younger Elijah for whom other names would be found, when he had discovered Gourd the arrow-maker stealing their eggs in the hen shed. He had cried out, "Gourd steals from us. Gourd takes our food," and had run at the man, his small arms flailing.

Gourd was a man bear, and he grabbed the boy by his neck and lifted him toward the moon. The boy could see the moon's light in the thief's eyes and could smell the grease on his body. He could smell the white man's burning water on Gourd's breath and feel the iron in his hands.

"You Elijahs are no longer of the people. You are kin only to the lizard and the spider. I spit in your face and in your food. I will reward myself with your chickens. You are washed in shame."

When he threw the boy against a woodstack, Gourd cast the eggs after him, and they broke open, their wet suns running on the boy's hair and chest. The smell was flat and ugly, and pain sparked through his back. He strained to attack again but could not rise.

Years later he could still remember the sound of Gourd's laughter like the panicked gabble of a jake turkey, and he was weighted down with pain when the man took the two hens in his fists and jerked them lifeless.

"I will devour the birds of the outcasts and pray for their weakness," he said and turned to the moon, which seemed to give him strength and bathe him in its silver.

Then the boy heard a branch snapping and saw his father standing in the shadows with a hatchet in his hand.

"Stop him. Stop him. Gourd steals our chickens, father. He curses us."

But his father did nothing, and the arrow-maker raised his laughter to a cackle, then hissed like a snake: "He is in the spell of the Shawnee. He is a woman. Who will hear of my scorn for Not-Ross and his weak heart? Who will not find him a clown?"

When the moon raider had danced off with the chickens, trailing his triumph song, the young Elijah turned back to the man in shadows.

"Why do we suffer this misuse, father? Why did you not strike him?"

But his father turned away and said nothing, then went back to the hut where his tools lay in their rack and stared at the ground. Among other things, the boy long remembered the look of surrender in his father's face the next morning, the look of greasy water in his eyes. He could not understand why Gourd would despise them so or why his father would not defend his livestock or his son, and the memory became as a splinter, working its way deeper and deeper, far beyond skin.

Now a man, a Stayer, he hunted the people for the whites to drive them away like cudding cattle. When Captain Lawson told him a stalker could remain in the Shaconage and not be shipped west, could receive reward in exchange for captives, he nodded, and the bargain was struck, though he knew it was a contract that came with peril. Perhaps, eventually, he could have the white's property paper for land. It was a foolish notion, this ownership, but they believed and abided by it, and he might learn to accept their rules and customs. Then he could belong. He might raise a fence around all his goods and dare anyone to cross his lines, and he might have guests also to sit in a circle and speak with respect, but what would become of his spirit?

Though he wandered far and became a dog of the woods, he could read both Sequoia's writing and the invader's when he chose to. He spoke their words as well as his own, and he must have chewed gall to make his tongue right for it, but even close to the soldier post he camped alone and kept his silence. He was still a Cherokee, though he collared and killed his people, and if his pursuit caused him some regret, he believed he was following a design, which he heard in the owl's call and saw in the print of a fox by the beaver stream. The world was changing, he knew, but the reasons were beyond him, and there was no one to ask.

About his fate after the death prayer, he had no illusions. *Gano hali-dothi,* the hunter—he had become that thing completely, but those who would be his masters paid him in gold coins and called him the Claw. He cared no more for the white man's name than for "Elijah" or the quilled marks of his own nation's alphabet. He did not speak of family. He did not sleep in the whites' inn or blockhouse but kept to the borders, the dark margins. Nor was it the gold coins with their stamped eagles that provided his purpose. General Scott had said the mountains were crowded, but everyone knew raw ore had been found in what they called Georgia, and whites were determined at last to force the move they had long desired. These men ruled no true man's heart, but were only servants to a barren dream, and he would never allow them to hear his song.

He washed in sorrow and served only the bitter craving, straying far from lantern light and the comforts of a tight roof. When men asked why he kept separate, he said there can be no why, no reason. The world is an ambush, a mantrap, he had learned early, and he but one of the hammers that fell and fell as the world turned. The white stalkers were not scarred by the scoffing and taunting of their own people, as he had been, nor did they hear the wind's mocking and the warnings spoken long ago by Heron Woman. Nor could they ever grasp how a boy's confusion can turn to bile.

When Captain Dawson came to his fire to ask for coffee, the white man squatted Indian fashion away from the smoke and spat tobacco into the low flames.

"I reckon I understand why these skins don't care to leave the hills, and I can figure how you might be keen to stay yourself, might be willing to catch some and get you a pardon, but what's got me curious is how hard you go at it. Not that we mind, not that I mind, but you make a lot of enemies, you bring back a lot of hands."

Dawson had been a bounty man himself and had faced blades and arrows often. Spots of his head were bald, and his beard was a clump of swatches. "Close brushes," he told men. "If you're not mindful, bad things will come for you." He wore a beaded sash with two pistols and was known to spend his money on cards and harlots. The captain peered hard at the hunter from under the brim of his hat.

"You must have some hellacious score to settle with somebody."

The hunter kept his eyes on the fire, then lifted the coffee pot. "You want more?"

When Dawson declined, the hunter poured the dark liquid onto the coals.

"Some fires will be drowned, but there are others that run under the earth, under the roots forever. They will not go out, though their flames are unseen. It is time for sleep now, Dawson. It is time for a man to look to his own gear and his own reasons." Then he rose and kicked dirt onto the hissing embers.

In his blanket, he looked through the hickory limbs at the stars, where other people were hunting and carrying on ceremonies. They were wrestling or laughing or passing a basket of apples from hand to hand, weaving a marriage hammock or watching deer feed. Those who lived in the sky were all one tribe, moving on their appointed rounds with no interference, and he believed it was a life without pain.

"Perhaps," he thought, spurring his horse up the trail to Where Snow Waits, "Perhaps I too will soon find the place of rest."

When the sun came up, his ground was scraped clean, and he had vanished. Not even Dawson could find tracks, as if the stars had carried the hunter off.

The ones who escaped him, who caught the scent of his smoke or heard his weapons echoing soon enough to clamber into the trees or scuttle among the tunnels they had dug near the sycamores of Singing Stream, did not dare attempt an ambush. They knew of too many who ventured it— Yellow Face who had leapt from a tree limb only to find his throat opened by the knife blade; Archille Smith and his father who grazed the bitter wolf with a lance but were run over a cliff by the big red horse; Andasarach, who carried only a stone hatchet and lost his face to a rifle ball before he could raise his revenge cry. And though the Bitterwolf dispatched the first few with regret and a shame that twisted his dreams, he soon learned to embrace his commission and turn his heart from the sun. Then there was only the pursuit and the quick fury of struggle, and then rest.

This rogue soldier who traveled alone and wore the white man's frock coat the color of night and boots with star spurs, the brim hat and trousers of twill, and who carried himself with the resolve of their traveling preachers, grew ruthless and keen. His shoulders were broad and his neck the girth of a bull's. His hands were larger than poplar leaves. He was a tracker more accomplished than Yellow Eyes, the panther, but he did not dine on what he slew. He carried or dragged the bodies to the bottomless cave near Eye Mountain, the endless Eye itself, and he flung them in with few words and no prayer bundle to accompany them. Sometimes even women in their tear skirts, for in a thicket, across a misting stream, in the green hour of twilight, who can distinguish?

Some had heard he clubbed the young ones as well, for pleasure, though many he brought back in irons were sons and daughters, who were light to carry and had little history with the land. Those who felt his blade or hissing bullets he dropped into the hole and listened as their limbs brushed by deep roots or thrashed against the sunless jutting stones. As they found the bottom and met the mystery, the sound scarcely reached the entrance. He kept a hickory spade in his cache under the ledge where the mountain came down to drink, and he shoveled some dirt and rolled stones in, as if he were filling the vast channel that led to the earth's center, to close off the seeing of the Eye. At least these people were buried in their sacred mountain. They would not suffer the displacement and rage and might rest in the Great Other. Perhaps even his father could finally sleep if all those who had shunned him were led to suffer. He strove to accept this burden, the fierce price of keeping his freedom, but though he showed no signs of regret, the wound he gave himself was deep. Claw. He was, to the Stayers, simply a mad animal. Some even whispered that under his britches was a wolf's tail, and his eyes at night were as lamps.

Those in the west who had survived the Trail Where They Wept knew well of his labors, his vengeance without mercy. They said it was not surprising, since his father had defied the elders. They knotted the rope against him and spoke to his father's ghost to scold him. They did not consult the Jesus or act in this matter as a civilized tribe, but spoke from a distant time. They cut their arms and offered their blood to moonrise. They held aloft the long, uncoiled body of *inadv*-the-fanged and asked him to strike the Claw when he crossed a fallen log or rolled in his blanket after eating *kanuchi*. They prayed *inadv* would not shake his tail in warning but strike like an arrow, yet they were never answered, for the new god brought by Worcester who built the mission blotted out the old ways, and that god would forgive anything, even for the Claw, even murder, even unbridled treachery and scorn.

How he found the hiders everyone wondered. He did not know the sacred words for many things, but he would ask Ancient Red to give him the breeze, and what he had learned in his boyhood rovings they could not know. He had spoken to finned things and winged ones, to the eyes that glare in darkness and the crawlers under the soil. His sweat had no odor of man, and his footfall was like the dropping of a feather. Even the red horse with its hard mouth had learned to walk with ghost softness, and his eyes were a spirit animal's amber. The Claw knelt amid the buckbrush and blackberries, the sumac with its red staghorn of bird fruit. He knew a bear scrape from tush hog's, buck's or the scar of an iron tool. His nose was a trail dog's, his ears the owl's, but some believed the wren messenger who could fly anywhere must have been bringing the Claw news of each movement in the oak woods, amid the spruce fields, along the tumbling streams from Ravens Washing to the scorched and scabbed landscape near Santeelah. They believed he was sent by Stone Coat who brought death into the world. Blessed by Heron Woman and summoned by the blood spill, he and his stalking song were from beyond the known.

Once in the fort, he had met a Tuscarora woman who worked at cooking for the soldiers. She was standing under a brush arbor, hanging fresh ducks amid other seasoning game. Claw watched her motions, which were fluid and graceful. Her hair was glossy in the sunlight, and her face was without scars and fair to look upon.

"What are you called?" he asked as he moved toward her, but her eyes grew large at the sight of him, and her actions lost all rhythm.

"You are the Claw?"

He could see she was frightened, and when he opened his arms, his hands empty and fingers outspread to show he meant no harm, she spoke something in her language, and he could read the tone, which was terror, and she was backing away, almost stumbling. She had no more wish to know him than the children of years ago in the village near his parents' cabin. If anything had changed, it was the fear in her voice, but that at least was something. That, he thought, was what he could claim.

Because he had been an outcast, the Claw knew where to seek those who had fled from Setsi and Tuckaseegee, Spike Town, Qualla and Nununyi, even far Catatoga, all the settlements pillaged by raiders after the Cherokee had been shuffled away. Even on a blue-eyed day such as this, as he skirted a ledge and saw the Catawba rhododendrons like flesh blossoming, he did not think of the council house nor the school, the sharp ring of the church bell on a winter day. All he could hear was the chock-chock of his father's tools, then the endless scraping. He smelled the smoke from hornbeam, fir and maple in the dugout as the coals spread their medicine. He smelled also the village feasts and learned to rob their hives by moonlight, to know at least a taste of sweetness. He saw the other boys wiggling their skinny backsides at him and heard the words for *Shawnee* and *witch* and *whore*. Even under their caned roof the no-clans, the Bitterwolves, kept their talk to a whisper, eventually only the two Elijahs, as his mother was soon gone, and they never knew where. The boy lived and labored under a curse and kept his own counsel, as if knowing, as if seeing what will yet come as others see what has passed. He read the signs and followed flying things and those that crawl and those that dart and scamper. He had heard the stories and warnings of Heron Woman and learned the ways.

He was tall and ropy in his body with eyes hard as a pine knot. His shorn hair was concealed beneath the hat whose shadow kept his brow in darkness. The origin of the wide scar along his jaw was his secret, and he rode with no bead, no feathers, no ornament but the brass tacks on his gunstock, the bone gorget concealing a healed slash across his throat. The whites would say he needed a woman or whisky, needed to speak of his anger or settle in another land, but his aspect was so honed and rigid not even the boldest would smile in his presence or meet his gaze. They spoke to him and of him with fear and envy.

The Claw's father was never asked to sign the New Echota Treaty, but he came to council and spoke his first word to them in many years, forbidden, but saying anyway it was a death warrant for the people. They were putting their marks on the edge of the world, he said, shattering the circle. Again, he opposed the thunder of many voices. They dragged Elijah out and urinated upon him, then showed him their backsides wagging. They had thrashed him before and scourged the boy as well, but suddenly, as they dragged the Bitterwolf back to his garden the last time, they found a strong young man before them, an adze raised in his hands and eyes fiery, so they turned from their purpose and retreated to the council. And now they were dying in many ways.

On a day as brisk this one, under crows sweeping, does the hunter stray from his stalking to think of the misery he increases? His heart, he thinks, must become harder than a tortoise shell. He is armored in hatred he no longer strives to command. His father's face rides in the clouds above him, grieved and disapproving, but it is the habit of fury that urges him on, even with no family sanction. Bitterwolf, Claw.

His red horse is stout enough for the plow; he seldom gallops, only climbs steadily, almost floating. The pack mule has a blind eye and is the color of bear scat. The solitary hunter carries a thonged buck sack against his skin—garnet amulet with a fresh heart root, puccoon, the dry medicine and wet. In the distance he hears a woodpecker rattling. Ta-la-lah, brother hunter. He knows a fire rises from the bird's being, the burning soul. Ta-la-lah knows it is death which gives life to the darkness. He seeks his prey without heed for his own pain. He too must be branded with some injury that demands answer.

The man the Claw seeks now is Wilson Halfbreed who came from Turkey Town on the Coosa to these higher reaches, fleeing random constables and squads of government soldiers, leaving a conspicuous trail, though he's wary of these notorious precincts. He has heard many stories of the Cherokee manhunter, his stealth and might. Moving with haste and little skill, Wilson does not know he has already entered the realm of the

Wayah. Wearily, he kneels by a small fire at a cave mouth, but the trail of *tsugasvsdu* curls upward, smoke like the coils of *uktanah,* and the smell of his rabbit has touched the distant Bitterwolf's nostrils.

The predator's eyes darken with the shadow of hunting. He feels the quickening inside him, another chance to prove his power, his worth, if only in rebellion. After sipping from the silver flask that weights his jacket, he urges the red horse onward, over a stream where *aroughcan* pauses at his washing and glares through his black mask, fellow fisher, fellow skulker. The ground is uncertain with rubble and duff. The horse moves slowly. Nearby orchis flowers soften the hard place to the hunter's eye.

One night he removed the graying mandible of a horse from his satchel and scraped a peeled stick along the teeth, first in a pace as steady as creek water, and its clacking was the sound of a war rattle, but when he altered the rhythm, he found something he had learned from white man's music rising outside the circle of their fire. "Old jawbone," he sang in amused imitation, "the old jawbone." As he repeated the phrase and filled in where memory failed with sounds from his own tongue, he could almost hear the fiddle sawing, the lute's comforting chords, but he stopped abruptly and tossed the relic onto the ground. It was a song, but it was not his.

Lying back, he again recalled the picture repeated in dream after dream. The ambusher was always the same, Skin Woman, whose husband Yellow Thorn he had killed at the fight by the abandoned wagon. Yellow Thorn had eluded his reach for months, but the hunter discovered the family's cache below the berry hill and waited there. Seeing his pursuer haul supplies from behind his own buckbrush blind, Yellow Thorn had drawn a butchering knife, and with teeth bared and eyes glowing like mica, he broke cover and rushed at the hunter. Claw turned just in time to see the bolt of motion and feel the heat of fear. His Colt cleared the holster in its fluent way, without his thinking, just as Thorn reached him, and the report of the weapon had been muffled by the belly it was pressed into.

Claw had escaped the blade, but worse than the wound he might have taken that day was the blow the wife would strike later. She had been hiding beyond the bluff and knew from the pistol shot what had happened.

Though Claw scoured the vicinity, he could not find her niche, a sinkhole covered with fir boughs and clots of moss. Though he passed close by, she held her breath and never moved.

Though her stone had just grazed his head on the evening when she found him, he still had spells of dizziness and wore a crown of pain. His vision would grow dim, and lights danced before him like shooting stars. The pain would set upon him suddenly and just as suddenly vanish.

He should never have been so careless, even in the shadow of the fort, but she was light-footed, and the people said her heart was already dead with the loss of her husband. She was wind-lifted, and though she had sojourned briefly with her husband's people and seen to the cleaning of Thorn's handless body, though she had rent her clothing and sawed off her hair, her mind was on the man who brought her husband to his death. That is what the stories said, but the hunter had not heard them in the margins where he moved. He was still outside the circle.

She lived on roots and forage from the garbage pits, and some had believed they saw a face in blue paint shifting through the shadows but dismissed it as an apparition. She was confident the hunter would capture others and come to collect his bounty. She knew he would return, and she waited. In the shadowed hollow of a great rotted-out hemlock, she did not sleep and kept an eye trained for the hunter, for some had claimed he spread his blanket nearby.

He pressed the heels of his hands against his temples to smother the falling stars behind his eyes, but he could still see her in the twilight as he walked toward the spring for water. The camp was still, noises from the tavern rising, and she sprang from the rotted trunk with the blade in her teeth, a white cross painted over her face, one stripe down through the nose, the other across the eyes, blue skin behind them, and the rest of her form was without clothing, blue-stained and sheathed in filth. Before his back touched the earth from the shock of the flung stone she was upon him, her breathing a raw, hungry sound with a scream cutting through it.

It was the same knife, her husband's, long used for butchering sheep and the white scut deer that fell to Yellow Thorn's bow, and it slashed Claw across the shoulder and dug into the earth so that she could not free it for another blow.

The hunter was certain that a ghost was upon him. A dark wind had rushed him, and he brought his hands forward to receive it just as her blade ripped his jacket and flesh.

They rolled in the dirt, kicking and striking each other. Darkness was closing, as the sun had fallen behind the rim of Goathead Hill. His cheek was grinding into earth, the green pine needles with their scent of life and the dead cinders of an old cooking circle. The body upon him was wiry as smoke but strong and greased. Her teeth were slashing, arms flailing. They pummeled and thrashed. Over and over they rolled, gouging and choking, and the hunter believed this thing fallen upon him was a curse thrown by some spell caster. He remembered wondering how a spirit could have such writhing weight and solid form.

At almost the same moment, they ceased struggling to draw breath, and he knew that the being he pressed to the earth was human, was a woman, her body scarred and scraped, her hair shorn. Then she kicked out and rolled again, straddled him, grasping his neck, pressing the thumbs into the apple of his throat. The world was going darker, and he thought he might accept this as the ending. But just as his breath weakened, a rifle cracked. An Iroquois in soldier uniform was standing just ten feet distant, and the force of the ball lifted her and threw her back against a broken wheelbarrow.

Later, the white healer's tonics had roused him, but they left a bitter taste. When he woke in the camp cot, he was looking at a porcelain bowl with a black rim, half of it in shadow. Then the color of cured deer hide blocked his sight, and he could make out fringe moving and a bead pattern on britches. A shadow fell across him and the voice said, "Sawbones says you'll get through it," and, "Damn, fellow, you shorely do know how to make a woman mad."

The troopers threw her naked body into the pit with those taken by the milk sickness, but Tolbert Winston told him she was Yellow Thorn's woman, who had vowed to be his destruction. He added, for no clear reason, "Did you know her ma was white? She was a mongrel, boy, and she like to took your blood."

He felt a chill of shame crawl up his spine. The woman they had killed, who had nearly succeeded in sending him to the beyond, was a warrior, a Bitterwolf like himself, but those who had rescued him were no better than yard dogs, the curs who cringed for the white man and carried his burdens and licked his hands.

Last night the Claw leaned against a deadfall's root-clump by a trout pool near the Speaking Shelves and feasted on his catch. His bow drill and sparkboard lay on a flat stone. His coat buttons shone where he had hung the garment on a cedar snag. The taste of the fish was cleansing, and he ate it the white way, dusted with pepper, salt, shreds of cress from the mud bank, dust of amanita. Then he gave the bones back to the river, for some bargains must be kept. When he looked up through the trees to Sky Mother, whose ceremonies he had long refused, lights from the High Boys sparkled across the sky like so much spilled salt. Once, he would have loved to carouse under their protection with others of his kind. Now he only wished for power or the Great Other and the peace it might bring. He rubbed a salve of boneset, possum grease and cobweb on the injuries not yet healed over, the long scar across his shoulder, the palm scraped by a stone. These, he knew, were not signs of achieving peace. The only sure future is the black threshold and death.

His pistol needed cleaning, the intricate works and hinged trigger oiled, and his carbine could use a fresh cap on the nipple. His ramrod cleared any grime the day had sifted into the muzzle, and he stared down into the barrel's maw, then dry-patched a ball to secure it in the breech. The hole was darker than the Eye, where some said his ancestors had emerged to enter the spinning chaos of the Nantahala. It never seemed a place of beginnings to him, but only the agent of ruin, which lurked and cowered in every rift and fracture of the spinning world, for this is the road an outcast follows. The old stories were full of renegade tales, how the shunned one would triumph, but he had ceased to believe them and now followed the crooked path, for it was what he knew.

He knew, also, he must always be at the ready, even in camp. He must imagine those like Skin Woman and keep them in his vision, but after briefly looking to his weapons and rubbing his hands against the evening chill, he chose to unwrap the flute from its sheath of trade cloth. He ran his hands along the smooth shaft and caressed the locustwood turtle his father had lashed to its length years before. The hunter flexed and stretched his fingers, then touched the blow hole to his lips. Was it the song of Strawberry Woman he played, or the lament for Crazy Snake, another outcast who had fought to save Jackson at Horseshoe Bend? That man had been accused of stealing by the Americans he served, then hanged from the white man's gallow tree. His song was grief unrelieved. It was loss and thirst for belonging to more than a place. Perhaps the tune he blew into the long bone was a plea for some end to his madness, to his wandering across the blurring mountains, the loss of what he never owned, or it may have been just a wolf melody. They too have their music.

The notes rose beyond the spruce tips and tulip poplar. They soared on the wind, then dipped into a gorge to fade into another realm. Perhaps the Heron Woman or some other prophet of splendor and doom heard them beyond the valleys. If the Heron Woman was listening, would she hear in it the wish to be beyond all this killing, to fade into groundfog or be called back to his father by light from a wandering star?

When the tune was finished, he looked again to his weapons. Then the nighthawks flaring through the narrows above could hear the rasp of his steel killing knife across a cold stone, and they swerved, went another way, almost whispering their high cry. Perhaps he wished to be afraid in order to feel less alone. He knew a man summons ghosts as much with his working mind as with sleep, and ghosts can bring the destruction that is without release. He sipped at his cup of persimmon coffee and watched the coals go white as winter. His father, edging axe and adze, had told him the metal must not reach the color of snowflakes but should be hammered red, and never struck on the edge. That way the tool would retain its temper. That way what was meant to cut would not shear off and be ruined. It would be stern as the heart of a devoted man.

As the Claw slept under an overhang of gray rock, Wilson Halfbreed crossed a meadow and entered a stand of black gums, moving slowly. He tripped over woodbine and heard wild ducks flying low. The sound terrified him. Panting, he rested in fetterbush but did not know it by its smell. He scrambled on rimrock and saw the sun climbing above the valley smoke and fierce green of candling trees. If the sun had looked back, it would have seen his face painted strangely, for it resembled a lowland parrot bird, all pigment and startle. His head was wrapped in a head-dress of willow sticks and turkey quills, and his hands were covered in yellow dye. An amulet dangled with his privates. In this guise he might travel at night without fearing spirits, and he felt stronger this way, his jake feathers hanging to his shoulders, a third eye drawn pale as the moon on his forehead. He cupped his hands before him as if to catch rainwater, but what he drank was the new light. He was greased to give no human scent. He knew anything moving was his enemy. He would bring death back into the world with his bare teeth and nails of his fingers, if need be, before they would manacle him and drag him into the flat places to the west. He listened to the cry of some small creature in the brush and shook his rattle, corn in an orange gourd, the sound of courage. And yet he was afraid.

That morning, the day of the woodpecker and the quickening, under a sky blue as the half-breed's eyes, the hunter must have been thinking he might soon have another body to cast into the pit under Eye Mountain, another palm of bright coins that gave little pleasure but possessed small music of their own. He could feel his path and his prey's converging. He had not even thrown the sack of shackles into the mule's panniers this time—keeping his kit simple, knowing it was only a solitary he pursued, not even a person from this range, as he could read by the clumsy trail, the scuffs and twig snaps, discolored leaves even in the open along the old runner path. One more coup for his father and the Shawnee woman he could scarcely remember. One more note for his own flute song trying to erase the past. And yet, he knew one who holds death in his hands must remember it can slip loose at any moment.

When the sun was high, he cocked one knee around the horn of his saddle and perched as he ate dried squirrel, then gave his animals a hand-ful of corn and drank from his gourd. If he had family, he thought, this was it, the three of them seeking a reason to rest, a place of clear water, a moment for release. The trail was colder than he had expected, the clues less obvious now. Perhaps this Wilson was not one who travels alone. Guardians chose their favorites at random. The hunter did not know his quarry's totem or clan. What would be his habits, his prayers? Passing a sweet thorn shrub, he startled a flurry of birds and greeted them, watching as they scattered and vanished.

Opening his spying glass and turning with one hand on the cantle, the Claw swept his lens over witch hazel and wild grape, wind-tipped evergreens, then beyond, across scarp and rimrock and peaks washed in watery light. Everything he scanned was larger but less clear, more swirled in the great mystery. He was weary and not cautious, the eye of his glass flashing the sun's message back across the gorge, where anyone with a keen eye might have seen. On his wrist he felt a slight motion, and when he looked down, a speckled tick was about to crawl under his cuff. Flicking it away he thought, blood drinker, never-quenched, a bad sign. But there was no time to take measures against it, as the horse snorted, shook its withers and pawed the earth where the footing was unsure. The trail here verged on a steep and rocky drop. This was not a safe place to pause or think of threatening medicine. There could be no safe place. He drew the left rein taut and pressed his knee into the animal's side. Hyah. And they moved on.

Afternoon passed to evening but left spirit shapes of fog in the low places, almost as warnings. His eyes swept the undergrowth and drying rocks but found nothing disturbed. Downhill, carefully, toward a lower ridge, his small caravan traipsed, their full energy devoted to caution. Below he found water moving and the thinning light tattered by new leaves, but the only sounds were the clop of his animals and the creak of tack, a few insects answering. No matter how much he worked it, he could not rub the noise from store-bought reins and girth strap until they had wintered in the hills, though his old saddle was quiet as moss. He watched wrens in the pawpaws and listened for the underworld that lived beneath streams. A speckled bird thrashed and fluttered from cover amid weeping ferns, and he had come to a place once called Otter Sleeps. The Claw dismounted and drank from a riffle by sips, then ate an apple, perhaps thinking that his daily need for food proved he could not be from the other side, though his feelings were still and cold and almost without flavor. Even the apple's tartness translated as bitter or bland or nothing at all.

He would find the runaway, he was certain, near the rock called Where Wolves Shouted, a good breathing place, headwaters of Swift Creek. Perhaps this one would be easy to capture and present no problem to transport, as the early trail had suggested his quarry was no woodsman. Or perhaps, the Claw thought, I could just allow him to travel on. It was not a foreign impulse, and it amused him, but it passed. He filled his gourd and swung into the saddle just as the red horse's ears twitched with caution. He took a deep breath and smelled sweetness, then stood in the stirrups to pluck a magnolia petal, the *wahoo,* which quickly rusted and went limp at his touch. He swung down and relieved himself against a black oak, and there felt the pounding again in his temple, the message left by Skin Woman's stone. He wavered, and the limbs above grew blurry, dreamlike, but it lasted only a moment, and he rode on, uphill again, the steep way treacherous with shivery light failing.

On the switchback, a defile brimming a sheer ravine forced him to lend the mule more slack and scour the trail for solid footing. He leaned away from the mockernut grove to study the stump of a sawed tulip tree whose whorls told its good years and lean, the story of the forest, and the clean cut said canoe wood, a push-pull saw. But why on this cliff so far from the big river? he wondered. If the prophets had been wrong and the Georgia gold not poison, he might yet be a man making boats under a sacred hemlock, creating vessels and hunting the generous-hearted deer, though that labor, too, would have been his alone, his father dead already these two winters. The circles in the stump seemed a whirlwind's silhouette, frozen, almost a target, a sign. Again he felt the pain as it moved forward to his brow, but he blinked and shook his head. Doubtless the ache, as usual, would soon leave him. A kind wind would carry it off.

That was when the hunted man—unheard and unsmelled, appearing from nowhere—flung a cloud of mushroom dust and leapt from behind a jutting rock like the hunter himself. Brandishing his cudgel and rattle while he screamed like the panther, like a woman in labor, but attacking, his face something fierce from the old stories, his motion strong, awkward with desperation. The red horse reared as its rider strained to steady him. The forelegs kicked air, and the mule sat back on its haunches and brayed in fear.

The reliable carbine failed him then, the misfire discharging an impotent smoke plume that hung in the warm air, its scent acrid. The report was hollow. Branches slashed at him, whistling, and with the horse he spun. Now the ragged clown in cloth trousers and a blouse, but with the face of a bird demon, collided with the unbalanced horse, shoulder to flank, and as the Claw strove to pull the Colt from its holster, thumbing the hammer back as he drew, his alarmed mount threw back its head and barked, then bucked like a hooked trout, moving with no awareness of the nearby precipice. The Claw struggled for balance, and as he heard the wind whip and hammer while the strange figure, the bird warrior thrashing like madness itself but striking no skilled blows, continued to scream and wave its limbs, which rustled like flailing wings.

The mule was trying to back along the narrow edge now, its halter lead loose and giving no guidance. Its one good eye could see little of what transpired, but what it saw must have been awful, a mule's horror, all speed, verve and contortion. It could smell the disorder and sense the confused bodies moving. It bared its teeth and honked goose-fashion. The hunter cursed in Cherokee, falling back on his source of First Words, while his mount slipped on chaff and scree, humped itself to recover, then shook its great muscles, bucked again and tried to bound away from the bright figure, but there was no ground there. The earth had ended, and both rider and bewildered horse launched into open air and began to tumble slowly, as if the confusion would not allow time to move forward at faster than a crawl. Their movement was dreamlike, as when the shot pigeon is whirling, wing-braked, but still falling. So also was the mind of the Claw stunned and spinning.

His thoughts swept from the shaken backsides of his boyhood tormentors to the faces of his prey, both alive and afterward, to the grotto of bodies, cold fire rings, the dishonest circle of a white man's hammered coin. His father's face, grim with sorrow, hovered before him, followed by the streaking tears of many ancestors, bewildered at what they had seen. The grimed face of Skin Woman looked down from a cloud and sneered, and in that instant he knew all was lost and the road come at last to its ending. He felt his body grow lighter, his arms unencumbered and sleek as wings. Eyes shut and muscles all releasing, he gave his song to the wind and to the memory of his father's smile over the first rough dugout the Claw had carved.

No image could buoy him, however, no wings formed, and he knew he would never regain the earth that had been snatched away. His eyes turned skyward to see the cold sun, and he felt something, perhaps a feather, brush his forehead, as if blessing, as if anointing. Then he was bouncing, careening with broken rocks and limbs, was smashed twice against stone edges by the horse's struggling body, and then there was no wolf howling anywhere nor hawk squalling nor any sign of mastery or magic, no song from the spirit world or the medicine cast in his amulet, only the aftermath of dust and the first spits of cool rain. Then nothing at all but the stalled mule's bray on the ledge, though the Claw could not hear, though it might echo through the night from Qualla to Tuckaseegee, along the river and up the steeps.

The fugitive lay on the edge breathing hard, a fire in his chest. He stood slowly and spat blood as he peered over the rim, still trying to grasp his good fortune. Both beasts were bawling now, the horse snarled and broken, a hundred feet below, its voice thinning to a whinny, the mule answering in terror. The man could not stop his hands from trembling, and the front of his trousers was dark with his own water.

The hunter's black hat had rolled downslope the farthest, a dark wheel now still amid the suckle vines, its crown torn, and already a raven had reached the motionless body, pecking at the flesh that had been the Claw's face. The rain squalled in, smelling of dust and pollen, rattling the twilit leaves, but ceased as quickly.

Wilson Halfbreed raised his painted face to the east where the new moon was rising, barely visible, the red rim of a shut eyelid. Still astonished at such luck, he whispered thanks to Heron Woman and the Invisible Others, any guide or benefactor he could name. Down the ravine were weapons and other supplies to aid his journey. He cast a handful of rubble at the carrion bird, and as it ascended, it laughed in its bitter tongue. The raven wheeled and drifted and delivered, again, its broken song, while the man shouted skyward, as if he might be heard along the ridges from Junaluska to the Shining Lake and all along the High Country of Great Smoke, even beyond the stream Where Wolves Howled, as if in blessing, as if in defiance of all the world's hunters. Then Wilson Halfbreed breathed deeply the flickering twilight and slowly began the perilous climb down.

Blaze

Dreama won't visit now on account of the accident part. That bitch. So on visitors' afternoon I just watch dirty shadows the window bars make across the wall of my cell. There's voices all over the prison, penitentiary they call it, all the whispers. The sun's a fire, we know that. It's the dragon, and Lord, I love it, but not from here.

They caught me because I had to watch. It's like somebody snatched me around and said, "You can't look away, you can't leave." Under the streetlight, why didn't somebody else look like a burner? I shouldn't've lit the church where I was working, I know, shouldn't've kindled up my own nest, but every day I wondered what shape the flames would make. They caught me quick. They didn't even wait a minute to click their silver-colored cuffs on my wrists. I couldn't feature that, how they'd just look in my eyes and know. "Arsonist": That's their word.

She got the waitress job at Howard Johnson first, day shift, and I stayed home studying Regis and Oprah, but I had the itch to get out. West Virginia was weeks and miles behind me, an empty warehouse on the edge of town, a bad memory I was growing past, a habit I was free of. I sat on a hill by the railroad ravine on that last Wheeling evening and saw the useless wood burning up to heaven. I had a job washing filth from cars on a lot. I bought her the scarf so red it could have beat a fire truck. It all comes back to that. She packed us up, slamming things around, and said, "You couldn't stop yourself. I understand. Next time, Elton, you got to keep telling yourself, 'I won't, I won't.'" She'd tickle me and make me laugh. She might've almost been my sister, we were that close. I needed somebody to remind me: Old warehouses are a trap wanting to be big hawk-feather flames, waiting to lure me in.

When she found me, I was living in bins. My brother stuck a candle in the mule's skull and tapped on my window. Scared me to death. Travis in the paint store paid me a dollar to touch his thing. That was bad. Fire jumped in flower colors, daffodils and violets, in our gas heater that hissed. Behind the glowing shields, the dragon was keeping us from freezing. Tommy and Dub Stevens said pissing on the volt fence would make you feel good. When I arced my water, a light knocked me out cold. I was scorched. My daddy never spared the strap. When Mama hit a rattlesnake with the push mower, bits went all over like sparks. How I stepped on a fang nobody could tell, but I upchucked and went into the fevers. Mama put the onion on it, then ice, and it burned me, changed me, made me strange, the lawyers say. Fire is free and nobody beats it, so I lit out, lived on my own till she came along.

Dreama's manager Mike Brattle set it up, the Last Chance Baptist Church needing a night cleaning man after the choir practice and prayer meetings, the youth groups and mission committee and Bible study. I liked all that. I wore the orange coveralls like somebody hunting, working in the woods and being safe from rifles. My name on the pocket and people coming in to say "Howdy," but I mostly had the place to myself, and I could make it shine. The colored glass sometimes caught some light that made it look afire already, the polished hardwood near yellow. That kept the bad seed in my mind.

I liked him, though, Deacon Mike. He showed me the closet with mops and cleaners, all the rags I'd ever need. Linseed, bleach, Comet. When he wrote down what solutions went to solve what filth problems, I knew I had respect. He liked the "cleanliness next to Godliness" thing and said it a lot, but he never tried to save me from anything but goo and strong liquids that'd eat your skin off like an alien movie. So I was sorry for him.

I took a nap back where they kept the hymnbooks and old broke-up furniture till it was late. I already had my plan, the matches, the picture of a fire like an arch inside my head. I had to spill my coal oil along the hall and into the office. I had to get the heat high before anybody could see through a window that a wrong light was running, free as starlings, through the pews and up to the altar. I never knew he was still in there.

They said in court he'd stayed late to talk to some grieving lady in the basement, but that makes no sense to me. I can't be responsible. I lit it up. Red leaped like Dreama's scarf around her neck. "Scarf scarlet," the voice of the dragon roared. I gave it to her on Christmas and when we went out, the wind caught it up. What a dance it could make, silk tips like a snake tongue fluttering.

The smart part of me ran from the first licks of fire, slipped along an alley in the back, then circled, kept low in the dark, all crouched. The smoke was white against the sky. I never liked the sirens. They spoil it some. When the crowd commenced to cluster, I stole in among them, feeling blessed. That was when a man outline appeared on the porch, all trimmed in fire. He was dancing, shake and shimmy, a man-shaped flame. That's what they mean, "all robed in holy light." A lawyer said they had to bury him in a closed coffin. They made me carry the blame. Somebody from the choir out there in the street pointed me out, said what I worked at, told them my name.

Just a boy, I set my first one in a cornfield. The ears already picked. It would've been harmless, but it caught the woods and spread faster than any dragon I had ever seen. It made my skin prickle up. It was mine.

Anyway, that's why she won't come, the church all soot and smolder, the man turned into a crispy angel. I never meant that, but now all I've got to talk to is shadows moving up the wall. They could be smoke. When I close my eyes and picture up the first time, Conder's woods, all those pines gone to stalks of fire, it still gets me. I like to remember back, to feel how it was hackling on my neck, the goose bumps all along my arms. I can't unlove the thought of torching things to beauty, but in this crazy place of cold walls and strangers who'll spit in your food or jab you with a spoon, it ain't the same. They think they got me, you know, they believe they do, but I smell something sleeping under all this cement and rebar, something like the dragon. I'm getting the itch again, and I always know where to find a match.

Razorhead the Axeman

The hummingbirds have gone off for the night, and John Rose and me are under the catawba tree drinking co-colas, telling boo stories and writing our names in lightning bug jelly on a slate from the barbecue pit. It is good to write your name in fire, even if it fades quicker than the taste of soda, which you can never quite call up when you're in bed after your prayers. We have a whole jarful harvest, so we can do it again and again. When the letters disappear, we close our eyes and make like we're going too, escaping this sleepy-headed place.

John Rose wants to tell about White Face, who has possumy teeth and a snake tail. He will perch on your closet shelf and breathe the cedarwood till you open the door, then pounce, and he'll tear your throat out with his arrowhead teeth. I won't let him, though, because he told me that one just an hour ago when we were shoving the splintery old cover back over the well collar. Down in the cut where the Dovetown children go to eat clay, we can hear the train to Atlanta moaning, and it puts me in mind of Razorhead, who my cousin Ridley told us about last week. He was born with his face bones wrong, which made him grisly to look at, but he had a rare and wondrous soprano-kind-of voice. Something about how his mouth come together in a point at the front of his wedge-shaped head made notes blend together a way nobody else could make, and they kept him behind a curtain at church, where he sung "Gladly the Cross" and "Just as I Am" with such beauty people would swoon.

"He slew them in the pews," Ridley said. She is going to be a nurse, so she likes the sight of people needing aid.

"They fell out in a God-spell," she said, "women and children and strapping men. And when they come to, they was refreshed. Then the preacher would pass the missions pan, and wouldn't nobody hold back, as they felt blessed."

I am telling it now, adding my own details, and John Rose wants to know if Razorhead was his real name, but I ignore it. He can ask stupid ones sometimes.

"Then they would have to smuggle him out the back and into a truck with one of them French legionnaire caps backwards on his head with the little curtain like the kind the doctor pulls over in front of a person in the hospital that has died."

"Did he like his job?"

"Well, maybe at first, but he heard how other chaps was getting to go to the ice cream supper or maybe to a Crackers ballgame at Ponce de Leon Park, and he started harping on it. The radio wasn't good enough for him anymore. He craved company. When they wouldn't let him out with the others, his parents and all, that's when he started killing."

"Why didn't they catch him?" John Rose was trying to write Razorhead on the slab, but he couldn't get to the end before the starting letters winked out, and we were running short of bugs. Before Daddy went to Nashville, he told me how their lights was courting lamps, calling across the lawn and into the woods. They didn't want to be lonely, either.

John Rose is just seven, so you have to say everything direct to him. I pull the church key string and fish it out of my shirt so we can have another co-cola, and I tell him Razorhead's big secret. He can hit a note that will make people's heads split open, and he sneaks right up to the window where there's nothing but rusty screen between him and somebody he thinks needs the punishment. Then he birds out that note, and there's blood everywhere while he runs along the privet and under the chinaberry trees, out through the rows of cow corn on the other side of Mr. Langslider's hay road. Before long, he's slipped back through the crawl space and into the trapdoor under his bed. He has so much time alone he has engineered a prison camp escape passage, so he has other skills, too.

We don't usually get many co-colas, and Jeanette is always bribing me with the promise of one from her icebox. She lives next door and is somehow related to me through a second marriage, but she's not related to John Rose at all. He comes over from his Granny Johnson's to play, because she's too busy mixing Cherokee weed charms in the kitchen to sell, and her TV don't work either.

Jeanette works last shift at the mill as a hemmer. She's put more than one stitch in her own hand, though she's young yet and shouldn't be clumsy. Brand Maxfield likes to visit her of an evening. He brings a guitar, which I'm always surprised he can play on account of his big hands. Brand works late shift at the pickle factory, where I gather he mostly shovels salt and stirs the brine.

First time I met him I was chunking the mailbox, watching the clods explode in the slow summer twilight.

"What you bombing, sport?"

"Jeanette."

"Whoa, you don't want to kill the golden goose. You blow her up, I won't have a place to knock off a quick piece before graveyard."

I told John Rose that—"knock off a quick piece." We started picturing Jeanette with a missing arm or foot or just toes.

"She could sew herself back together," John Rose said, "just run a seam. It's like she's practicing already."

I hate her, though, and I don't tell John Rose this, but what she wants from me is kindly sick. Sometimes she has charge of me after Miz Hanratty takes off and Mama's not home from the drugstore yet. Usually she just lets me run about and mind my own business, but last month she gave me a sack of fresh divinity to pull off my shorts and shirt so she could draw me and get practice on the human form. She said she wouldn't put on no head, so people wouldn't see whose dingler it was, and she didn't put in the scar on my chest where sizzle oil sloshed out of the fry basket when I was a baby and Mama was turning the catfish.

One time I was taking a bath a couple years back, Mama soaping me, and when Jeanette come over with a cold High Life for Mama, I slopped down in the water so she wouldn't see my particulars, but my bottom curve must have been showing over the edge, 'cause she said, "I can see the moon rising on the 'rizon," and she and Mama laughed. Ever since then she's looked at me kindly cross-eyed, but I figured divinity was a good price to get if you were going to sell your exposure. I can recognize a bargain.

This morning it was co-colas. Mama says only trash drinks soda before breakfast, and trash seemed to fit Jeanette like a doctor's white glove, 'cause she does it all the time. She favors Sun Drop in the evening, and she even has some Dr Peppers lined up in the icebox like a choir. Ridley says their name don't make sense, cause there's no medicine in them, but that clock on the glass is a warning, on account of they have prune juice in them. That's what gives them the left-handed taste. And the clock means to keep your eye on the time 'cause when that prune juice hits you, watch out.

It was right hot when Delbert picked Mama up for work this morning, and there wasn't no dew. She said, "Don't cross the road and don't tell no lies. Leave the mail on the coffee table."

We don't drink coffee, but we have a table for it. Soon as she was out of sight, I went into the wash house and swiped out a bag of clothespins to be the wooden people for my green army men to ambush. After lunch, when Miz Hanratty said I'd had enough nap, I read a Perry Mason story and built a bird nest out of wild sticks and meat-tying string. John Rose came over and we played mumbly-peg with pocketknives and then had a tickle fight. He had to go on home for dinner.

Then I was putting sticks in the holes of dirt-dauber nests in the tractor shed. They make these hollow things on the planks that favor a mud pipe organ, and then they put eggs in there to make more dirt wasps. If you could stop them, you would. Jeanette said there was hummingbirds still sucking the red tube on her porch, and I could sit on the glider and watch them if I wanted, so I did. We was swinging gentle in the shade, but the sun was coming in at a hard angle. Two bitty green birds was scuffling over the one honey tit, their engines zipping the air. They are more fun to watch than a yellow dog, but she was painting her nails from a bottle that said "Bleeding Heart" and then blowing on them. She asked what I would do for a co-cola.

"Stand on my head. Swallow a hummingbird. Say the alphabet backwards Z-Y-X-W."

"I've got a better idea. You come in here now."

The screen door slapped behind us. I already hated her, but she was the keeper of the drinks, 'less I wanted to walk all the way down to Horton's, and there it cost a nickel.

"Perch there on the settee." So I did.

"I want to see how one of your fingernails looks with this red."

My eyes must have gotten big as pie plates, because she said real quick-like, "It will be like a Rebel soldier's after he's been holding up a friend shot bloody to hear his dying words."

Though I had once claimed to her such a thing had happened to me just after Shiloh, I was still skeptical, till she said, "Two co-colas. Just so I can see the color from a distance."

By the time she was finished I looked really stupid, even if I was the soda king of Senoia, Georgia. I was breathing like somebody had been in a fight, and I bet my cheeks was red as my ten nails, which I chew, though everybody says, "Don't." She wouldn't clean them off neither and kept tossing the polish remover high up in a keep-away. I am not tall for nine, and I couldn't get close.

"Isn't she lovely," she sang, "isn't she lovely."

I knew if Ridley saw me, I'd have the sound of *nyah-nyah* in my ears for the rest of my natural life, but she was having no mercy, and I ran out of there with my arms full of cold drinks.

"How did they catch him?" John Rose asks. "How did they know he was doing it if the people looked like a axe had hacked them but they never could find no axe?"

"That's just it, stupid. They didn't catch him. He's still out there, maybe down in Howerton's pinewoods or hiding out with Sally Soapsud on the overside of the railroad track, and he can sneak up quiet as a milk cat to your window, and all it takes is that one note he's saving that comes on the music page way over the actual bars, and it cuts through the air just above you and then down till you split, and that's all she wrote. You won't be around no more than the lights of your name written in firefly goo."

Then I realize I might have gone too far, because John Rose is beginning to whimper, so I prize open another drink and hand it over. He can't see the polish on my fingers, as I have siphoned gas from the tractor and scrubbed them off with the wire brush Mama uses to clean the barbecue grill. I'm sore around the edges of the nails, though, those white rims, and I am glad I have done in Jeanette for good. John Rose doesn't even wonder how I got all these co-colas, since he doesn't ask, but I can see myself like somebody from the outside, a witness or crime snapshotter, as I crept back into her house like Razorhead myself and picked up the coal poker, which is brass-handled and bright as fire. Fire is what you have to make in you to get yourself free of shackling things. It's silvery fire on the bumper of Brand's Mercury, and you can see the sunlight shocking green fire off a hummingbird's feathers, so I had my inspiration. She was stretched out across the junebug-colored sofa, studying a movie-star magazine and drinking a High Life with the pixie girl side-saddling the moon on its bottle. When she looked up, it was too late. I didn't even have a wild-pitched hymn note to sing, but I pulled the poker down real fast, and her eyes went egg-sized, and she didn't have nothing to say either. Then I left the mess for somebody else and went by the icebox.

I filled the brown sack on the floor with what I wanted, then met John Rose in the side garden where he already had a quart Mason with stars popped in the brass lid and a couple dozen fireflies in there like a swarm. He was wearing three like diadem rings and one on his forehead like some Hindusian.

"Hey, Tucker," he said, and he had this other-world smile on his mouth because he's always glad for somebody to mess around with.

The poker was still in my hand, and I said, "Tell you what," so we went to the pump house and threw it under the well cover for a secret. "Don't tell nobody till you see God in person."

I thought to myself there might be enough spider nets down there to catch it before it splashed, but I was wrong. We might be getting a taste of hammered-out iron and Jeanette's blood forever, but it might be if they don't know how it was done, they won't know it was me. That was me scheming, which I have always been pretty good at.

So we're sitting out there under those crawly sap worms on the catawba limbs. It's night and we don't know what they're doing. Probably tearing up leaves. We're trying to remember a shiver story we haven't heard lately, but then the real Jeanette wakes up from her sofa nap and comes out in those awful pink plastic curlers calling my name and something about all her drinks and telling my mama, so I have to stop make-believing and start planning again. Getting out of this place is harder than finding a hummingbird up where they tighten their jewel bodies at midnight. Finding one sleeping is something almost nobody gets to do, but I throw my green co-cola bottle into the corn, tell John Rose goodnight and start figuring how I can be the one.

Dear Six Belles,

Is you is or is you ain't my baby?" The way you six can rasp that out puts all the human pain *du monde* in syrupy words. It's jubilee sorrow you raise with your sweet beat and squeezebox chords. Experience is what I'm saying, *chères*, drinking life straight in a full-gullet world-thirsty swig. You've got it, and also me. It's our fate link I call the Fidele. Knowing life's trials and thrills has made y'all great, your chansons, your riffs on old ballads, your coonass delta grins and the down-home juicy boogie that makes concert crowds sway and shiver when you all take the stage. This new stuff, though, the gyrating and the bumpy-grind, is almost a crime against nature. I know: I have been your shadow. For years I prayed you'd catch top-forty fire with your modified chanky-chank, and now it has come to pass. *Brisk Witches, File Flirt, Spanish Moss*—every album pure platinum. Nobody can touch you, not Buckwheat, not BeauSoleil. Hallelujah and *bois sec.*

Since I am your premier full-time fan, your loudest howler, the single beau who owns every disk and poster, promo gimmick and Internet image, you should listen, darlings, to my urgent words. My doublewide is a shrine, you comprehend? When they handed out those three-foot plastic Six Belles crawdads at last year's Mudbug Fest, I got there pronto, and mine hangs from the dining-room ceiling like a piñata chandelier. Even my mama finally came to like it. Even the Catahoula we call Tabasco, who barked *sans pause* for two days when I brought my trophy home. The fringed satin sash Lola flung to the crowd after the encore of "Swamp Snake" at last fall's Levee Jazz Jump: It drapes my wet-bar mirror like a riverboat strumpet's boa, and I'm right now wearing the pink Six Belles ball cap you all signed backstage in Memphis. Labor Day. The Pyramid. Scarred old boy in the red rodeo shirt and Groucho glasses was me. Remember? Guitar picks, a flung drumstick, a Mardi Gras cup with a perfect lipstick kiss on its plastic rim. That one's Bijou. A sweaty Coors towel sweet Marie tossed offstage back in '98 smells yeasty when I unzip its grip-lock sack. I've been backstage. I've seen your dressing rooms and made snapshots. I've got *couchoots* you don't even know you've lost.

That's why I have the right to say this direct, *sans souci,* and besides I've been watching close, a kind of guardian eye. I keep my owl-view Bushnells on sneaky Marie when she wigs up and wears trooper shades to slip into the Piggly Wiggly for souse or the makings of étouffée. *Jolie Blon!* No need to worry, I've got her back covered, and any stranger comes close to her pink Ford pickup I call "Blush," he'll have to deal with sneaky me. Stealth is not the only skill the Fort Bragg army teaches a man. Even Vangeline when she clubs and trolls for dirty-boy rough trade—swamp rats and pulpwooders—she's never out on a limb. "His eye is on the sparrow," you know. I'm invisible and everywhere, T-bone *ange,* you understand. The Fidele!

This is why I've noticed there's been some slipping, there's been gimmicky backsliding and decline. I know Lola's scribbling her new tunes while floating in a sea of Cuervo Gold, and it's starting to show. Vangeline is missing too many rehearsals for carnal cause, and when was the last time Soeur Solange dragged her cute ass to a Terrebonne *fais do-do* to refresh her homegrown dance moves? She needs to touch her roots, to taste her past. I could show her how, though mostly I watchdog sweet Bijou.

But *doucement,* family secrets, no? These are not tiddybits I'd post on sixBellesringing.com (yes, *mais oui,* that's me), but we gotta take steps to stop the bleeding before the fan clubs catch on or reporters start nosing around. You need to hold the peak so you can lasso a passel of Grammy gold next year. You need to saw that fiddlestick and make the cat cry, pump those bellows on "Madeleine" the way you did when you cut the tracks on *Briar Ruse* up at Muscle Shoals.

Now me, I don't desire reward for my services, *rien,* the pleasure's in the gift, and I prefer the shadows, but listen here. The way Lola shrugs and churns with her wild blue push-pull fiddle, the rosin ain't flying now, the notes ain't coasting. It's a thin roux you're spooning up, ladygirl. You're crimping the chords, bowing broad and cheating on the break. You used to gather every mote of music from the air like a papillon shrimp net not missing a one, and I could cut a rug to that, fall in pure ecstasy, be your cult, but now it's a piddling harvest. What gives? I may know. I fear the answer true lies in the bottom of the bottle curling with the Mexican worm. It festers in the glitter and the tease. What the Fidele gonna do?

Sans doute you're going curious about who waxes so. *Mon Dieu,* I'm dying to explain. Pappy Ambrose told me it's never polite to blurt out opinions without you've made your bona fides, your *pie de grue.* Pappy Ambrose, the whisky man himself—before his portable moon still sparked in the back of the Econoline and blew him to heaven—picked the tater-bug mandolin, and Mama plunked a stand-up bass. Blood-simple, I know rhythm. The yellowhammer having at the cedar siding as I hunt-peck this e-mail up, he has sixty-two cadences for different moods, and I know them every one by heart. Yesterday in the rain I heard a fresh noise, so I slipped on the yellow plastic jacket I call "Jonquil" and slinked around the corner to see was I right. Sure enough, every third tap he was twisting his bright noggin sideways to scrape his beak and cajole a swish sound. I've heard Vangeline stumble on that lick when she's behind the drum kit, lay-ing out the beat and seeking flourish, but she's forgot how to lay back and let the natural rise. I fear she's starting to pose for her vocal solo and the photo flash long before Roxie's guitar rips crescendo and gives way to the human tongue. She used to shiver the pie-dish cymbal with her brushes like a woman in love with starlight, and she could ruckus the snare like a bucket of churchmice fucking, but now its just lick-and-a-promise and deep décolletage, which is a flaw in the program, *chères.* You gotta cher-ish the blue swell in the emotional ocean, give yourself whole heart to the Loosiana razzy dazz. You gotta put it all on the line, and keep your sweet parts to yourselves, else some spark lands in the powder keg: Ka-boom!

But I was talking about me, so you'd know. I can't let percussion exper-tise distract me now. Bio? I was born outside Iota in Acadia Parish, family of sugar growers farming thirds, bad to gnaw the cane sticks for sweetness till our teeth was arrowheads, bad to scuffle and keep a corn-mash still. We swung the machete and smashed the stalks to syrup—git mule, gee and haw, circle like the slow dance blues. Mama said, "Be a priest. You smart. The saved won't care you got scars from a kerosene splash." But me, I stuck to trapping pelts on the backwaters instead, brought mushrats in and frailed a little catskin banjo, but what I strummed up was no better than flat gumbo. I have the gift in my ears but in my fingers, no. Can blow a little mouth harp, though. I call my Hohner "Silver." Picked up that art camping out with Uncle Sam. Two years. Ranger, me. I can catch Spanish Bayou gators with my hands, *mais oui*. I know explosives and night raids, too. I am danger's front-row man. This is what you need to know: I can't endure to see good whisky watered, true music muddied with excess flesh, my mighty devotion sullied by you or numbnuts gawkers or even, in my worst moments, me.

Lacking the knack myself, I long studied how Chenier could make you cry and Kershaw kept the mad dog in his bowing just barely on a chain. After service, I chopped hogs at the blood barn till the stench of guts and shit and *sang* soaked my pores, the screams of the dying pigs spooking any music I aimed to summon. Went roughnecking on stilt rigs, helping reap the Gulf oil patch for Uncle Sugar. Had *grande discorde* with that boss, also, in the end, but welding out there in sea weather, I taught myself to yodel with the transistor earplug tucked in, even in the *gros* storm. When wind howls like a *fantome*, you know saving music has got to be pure-T pure.

Old days, I might slip down to a chicken fight in Cankton or over to Mamou for a bounce and shuffle and Allemande, even a little punch and pummel. *Dansez!* you know, but always what I had in mind was the private passion for native music, *chères*, the banner flag-waving of beaucoup Cajun melody, the stuff you're the keepers of, the down-home divinity spark. Up there on the platform in weather, under the stars like salt spill and the wind's spit whistle, the tunes, they'd keep me warm, and I loved the pop of my 'cetylene torch catching, the way it hissed to sweat the copper just outside my plexi mask. I'd burn a whirl of color on the pipe, an eye like the peacock's tail or oil spill on wet asphalt. You know, I understood what I was looking at—colors of entrails, colors of an artist, *arc en ciel*, bruise flesh, raw colors of the soul, the magic music y'all made at the get-go. Before the big money started rolling in.

Vraiment, you might misdoubt me, and I expect if you ask you might hear some scuttlebutt about how this raw-faced man has raised his hand in anger on one occasion or maybe two, but it was almost always an accident, especially with that Pentecostal at Tante Vee's four years back. I just meant to shove him gentle and make my spirit known, and even the judge agreed it was all a sad misunderstanding, tragic but accidental. A year of stamping tags at Angola, then two more on the shrink's sofa was not so bad, and I learned some things about me. My old parole officer—*Merde-la-tête*, I call him—he finally learned to dig the sound of the jambalaya jamboree I was preaching up. About the time he cut me free, you gals blossomed on the scene, and my life ain't been the same. The Fidele was born, and what with the Lafitte pirate booty Pappy Ambrose dug up and left us, I'm at ease to follow my interests, so to speak, unhampered, free. Mama finally shut up about my taking vows, so I became a full-time Six Belles pilgrim, twenty-four/seven, dedicated to the treasure you all were born to tend and share.

I am no freak, if that's what you're almost thinking, no pervert *loup-garou*. I have had more than one Days Inn midnight rendezvous and a heap of sweetening. That's why I could always hear the *charivari* in your fingers, the good-heart shining woman moan. Lola's "Zydeco Femme Zoo" is my all-time favorite song, and when you dropped that prissy Dora Dean and picked up Baton Rouge's own darling gold-tooth Bijou to rub the scrub board and rattle the spoons, darlings, then Six Belles was born for true. Every jock on the AM wanted your sides spinning day and night, Sunday to Sunday.

For me, though, night has always been prime choice. I'd cruise the coast road in my old red Ranger truck underneath late starlight, swig on swamp pop and listen to your tunes, thinking it the best sound since Squeezebox Iry LeJeune, but I just thought of you as young girls learning back then, just kids, since your voices were so bashful, like Dauphin Island deer. Not full-grown women at all, I reckoned, but an angel band. First time I saw you strut the stage with your razzy dazz, *mon Dieu, très chaud!* How could any mortal rogue resist? Ahhhhhh, you were cooking then, not cheap or slutty, but pure cayenne. I confess—and this goes deep—my gaze was not always exactly chaste, and that's a problem, *chères.*

Do you recollect that summer evening way back when you were playing Duhon's behind the chicken wire screen? Yeah, skinny paychecks, dangerous places, early days. I've seen them coonass riggers throw longneck

Buds and beg for crude Hank Junior honky-tonk tunes when you were giving them the best jambalaya blues, Soeur Solange raising her nasal wail while doubling down on the bull fiddle with its foxtail flag. Authentic whangdoodle, *chères,* the true thing. And Vangeline made them kettles rattle, but the rude multitude wasn't listening close to the bone. You were stirring up a brand new gospel, but the crowds was too rowdy, too many goons, trouble sure. If music can cool the savage beast with charms, it can also make him snarl, and Lordy, the fists did fly by midnight. Cue sticks and bottles. I fixed a couple of the loudmouths on my own. Be thankful for that fence and dedicated men like me. No: There is no fan like me.

Now I cruise the bayou with cottonmouth and cypress, a thermos of Old Crow Coke and toot my mouth harp bright as a casket handle. Hi ho, Silver! Still feeding Fidele, I sometimes think about skin. *Voulez-vous* hear my humble opinion? You've got to watch out not to wake the scaries, the goths and goons. All that wild hair and sweaty cleavage, the stilt boots, peek tattoos and pierce jewels. You're no Bourbon Street strippers or hoochy-kooch sideshow, ladygirls. You've got to keep it under wraps, not show so much. Don't drag our music down the sleaze highway. Queen Ida never changed the music world with *tetons.* It was her happy weeping notes. And nobody in Cliff Chenier's entourage did the dirty shimmy, so tone it down. Scrap those bustiers and lace gloves that make you look like Hollywood rockster sluts. Stick with the ear music, *s'il vous* please.

My blood is up. You see, I've heard the rumors, how *Playboy* magazine has made a hefty offer to sprawl you out naked and make you rich as Huey Long. I'm warning: It could stir some trouble. I take it personal. Zydeco don't need exhibition or *beaucoup* lucre. It's all about tradition, that Fidele. Just play *piquante.* Keep those squeezebox buttons clicking, those strings and drumskins rousing for the cakewalk. Rip and run, but cherish the old-time cotillion undertone. You can sway us with "Diggy Liggy Lo" or a randy "Devil in the Moonlight," but don't cross over, don't go too vulgar, keep the *bontemps* stomp honest, darlings every one, for some of the spunky monkeys in your audience are not the safest kind of folks. I have seen behind their eyes. *Vraiment,* I myself am not immune to lower urges, and we don't want that *bête* set loose.

I sneaked off to a *traiteur* once and fed her questions along with bits of your lives—sun signs, hair locks, photographs and objects rubbed with your genes. *Chères,* she said the *couchemal* has a drifting soul and will haunt any native bayou girls who betray the people by going for the counterfeit and lazy. Said you have to proceed in caution lest some hex try to suck your breath at midnight, and not even the Hand of Glory, not Judas Root or Goofer Dust can veil you if you transgress, each sweet one of you. If the duppies come, you'll be gator bait or worse in a jiffy. Abide by the gris-gris, Belles. *Louche pas la patate.* The Prince of Darkness snaps at the heels of fame. He lurks and knows a fertile field. I would—I hate to say it— ease you to *le grand sommeil* myself before I'd let things slip that far.

I remember when you covered "Valsa Criminelle" following BooZoo's version. I could hear your throaty alto, Roxie, while your hands burned the chords crazy. Solange, you were scary with your basswork, calling up deep-sea catfish from chilly Gulf water and shaking ghosts from the soul. O Lola, so sober but wild on the fiddle. Marie finger-dancing on the keyboard and, ah, frenzy Bijou. You could already wake the sizzle in me.

It was like all the colors when I sweated copper with the torch, Vangeline conjuring the sunset rainbow rashing on the tap cymbals, and I surely fell in love with pure silk Bijou on the rub board, her fingers quick with their silver thimbles and catching every beam of light, an angel spreading wings across the bishop's altar. It was heaven's own clatter, but those days might be gone, and when I see some local fool at Solly's Dive or the Beer Barn pretend the nasty when you're on the video, I get like a firecracker, ready to boom the whole world. In fact, I had to get rough with one galoot, but you don't need to know how hard his fate came down, even if I did understand his hunger. *Gar ici,* sometimes you get even me thinking with my body, and that's a sorry state. So how we going to get back to the worthy kind of heat? How we going to recover? This is the urgent thing you need to answer. You see, *ma mère* has finally slipped from life this week, which leaves me a man alone and desperate to fend off life's bitter bite.

Right now I got novenas and chores to do, tools to whet, a hole to dig, a secret song to sing. I'm on a mission, *chères.* Now I'm an orphan in the open, and dawn is coming. I need to know.

Remember, next time you show down for a hoedown in the Big Easy or some rammyshackle parish hall, I will be out there like always, doing shooters and the treble Rebel yell, waving my Six Belles banner, rooting for you, with a pair of goggle eyes, a nose for news, a silky tongue, some scars I hope you can forgive. It's time we closed the gap, made contact. Bijou could comfort me so.

Don't drop the potato, babes; don't ruin the genuine sound we've worked so hard to keep moist and panting. And never let your sacred secret lover down. You know what's good for you. You know you owe me more than I can say, but what I have to whisper takes the form of warning. I need a dose of genuine swamp symphony to keep my demons on the leash. No more hoochy-kooch, *ecoutez-moi?* No more harlot clothes and tequila binges.

Let's keep this on the hush, in the family and make no *misère. Maintenant, laissez les bon temps rouler. Maintenant,* you never know. I could be closer than anybody's guess, close enough for a whisper, for a touch, *un baiser.* Yes. I could make a difference. I am the slow seep of fate's Fidele. *Vous me savez?* Don't y'all ever forget, now. *Au revoir,* till next time. Ah, *mon Dieu,* Bijou . . .

Tee Morceau LaLone

Little Sorrel

I shouldn't be telling you this: The bird that chirps always draws fire. Still, I was born to crow: The stolen mummy was in my garage all week. As you people out there in radioland must know, the police and newshounds don't have a clue, and the VMI brass are still dizzy with disbelief that anyone could hijack their favorite mascot artifact, could come by stealth and abscond with Stonewall's storied horse Little Sorrel. With impunity, I might add, and some panache. The dragnet is far flung, and TV news bulletins cast it as blasphemous, a modern atrocity, but I have reasons I'm certain tonight's audience is eager to hear. I have, in fact, permission.

I hope Madame Charlotte herself is out there listening and will at long last comprehend, though no one unassisted could have guessed my motive: following orders, respected rescue, instructions from beyond the grave.

He talks to me, you see. Not the general's trusty steed, but Jackson himself. Even when I'm cold sober. He's had my ear for nearly a year now, an eloquent old ghost, stern but avuncular, still a Christian gentleman. He wants Little Sorrel properly interred, no longer on display as a shaggy novelty or knickknack souvenir. As you probably know, what I purloined is not a normal taxidermied horse; they skinned the old veteran, tanned the hide and cast a base to stretch the pelt across. It's a normal approach to preservation, but in such postmortem operations size truly matters. It was no mean feat, I'm telling you.

The actual rusty bones were finally buried with ceremony under the moss-green bronze of Stonewall nobly pedestaled above the parade grounds, and the VMI boy-soldiers must surely wonder what any thief might want their equine trophy for. Not pelf, you must understand, not mere keepsake-seeking nor black-market profit. No longer a breathing creature, Sorrel needs to live in mystery and legend, grazing in meadows of the netherworld. He needs relief.

That's why I arranged this broadcast from the den that has served these recent months as an abduction situation room. The campaign is likely to come to a bad end, I know, but I want my story told, though I will conceal the true name of my accomplice, if you don't object, or even if you do. It's her job to perform the physical funeral, giving Little Sorrel his proper honors. So you see, I'm both the bona fide culprit and the decoy. It's a tactic I adapted from the Valley Campaign. I am confident you listeners will find this tale intriguing and see the justice in my actions, so keep that dial adjusted to capture my every word.

It starts in personal history. As a gangling boy I lingered in the parlor with glassed-in barrister bookcases and their treasures—Freeman's *Lee,* the Davis apologists, the whole war bound in luxury leather with gilt embellishment. Afternoons, I'd sip Mawmaw Paxton's peached lemonade and perch on the hassock fan. Absorbed, as they say. My favorite volume was always Henry Kyd Douglas: *I Rode with Stonewall.* That man was the proper cavalier, plume and spurs and saber, but trained to the law like my father, a man always drawn to the crucible, a knight of conviction and gallant fury. Even a day of carnage and snapping dragoon pistols in the face of frothing Yankees on the Sharpsburg Turnpike would stir him to say only, "We had hot work of it, and the song of bullets is no man's longed-for lullaby."

It's little wonder I soon delved deep into American studies up at the university, took two degrees, married and put my knowledge on the pedagogic market, then slowly rose to minor celebrity in a Roanoke community college. I write monographs and sit on panels. I've even been in the *Post* as a guest expert before. After all, the whole Old Dominion is consecrated ground and liable to inspire any acolyte with an inquiring mind such as my own. My class lectures on home-front duress, cavalry tactics and Lincoln's anaconda strategy were eloquent and animated, if I say so myself, and even from the weary secretaries and computer students in the back-aching desks, my passion always drew volleys of applause. Appreciation can revive you, but my dear Charlotte grew absorbed by her own career—engaged, distracted—so I sought validation from my profession.

That was all before, however, and it seems ancient history now. It was the reenacting bug that bit and nibbled me in secret, then opened wide to swallow my life. Quicksand, as you might imagine. I just wanted to be a hardcore foot soldier, tramping the land, keeping intervals, polishing and boiling and marching hard, debating the best way to fight blisters or keep musket cartridges dry. You know, shanks' mare, double-time, the whole low and authentic lot of a footsore private. "Arms and the man" I wanted to sing, to solidify my book-born theories and research with genuine hardship, to feel the camaraderie of the campfire and the heat of simulated battle. Can a recruit really "see the elephant" at all in a Saturday charade a century and a half too late? Even in his mind's private, active eye? I wanted to feel at least some facsimile of joy and terror. I yearned for purpose, fresh fire, the famous "new lease on life," or at least some earned fatigue.

I hoped to find it at New Market or Manassas Junction among like-minded men, weekend warriors with, perhaps, more energy than sense. A little weird, I admit, but not perverse. "Amateur" means one who does it for love. Do what you will and harm no one. Why not? Sometimes it was even fun.

My department chair Dr. Warren O. West, a syrupy-tongued Quaker from Georgia, encouraged me at first. His specialty is the history of medicine, and he thrives on describing field surgery and the astonishing effects of heavy ordnance on the human frame till his listener turns green at the gills. Trauma and body parts flung in the air are his fascination. If you chance into his office, you'll have to compliment his wedding-sized album of veterans with and without their ingenious prostheses and Gardner's grisly battlefield photos. A man with shifty eyes and some brush-on hair product blacking his squirrel-gray locks, he displayed the greatest enthusiasm for impersonation and bringing the past to life. He said, "Go on, enlist. Taste the black powder and parched corn." But he can't be trusted.

Charlotte, however, did not embrace this masquerade calling even from the start. I offered her the distaff option—hoop skirts, silk parasol and a peacock-blue flirting fan. She could have made a champion camp-follower, a darling Scarlett, a feisty Belle Boyd. She could have costumed as a nurse or even a transvestite gone-for-a-soldier gal. Instead, she turned her tongue sharp and cut to the quick every alluring thing about the Cause and my research aspirations. She would not, she said, volunteer for any *folie-à-deux*.

I had been dabbling for almost a year, acquiring from sutlers an appropriate forage cap, shell jacket, a replica Enfield and camp kit. No small investment. I'd even been through one whole day of a Gettysburg replay and had seen the lines of sweaty and overweight desperate men waver and fall, then witnessed their instant recuperation, which is the miracle that draws multitudes to this hobby: The dead can rise.

I was learning the ropes from the bottom up, happy just to maneuver and feign death and then dust off, take chipped ice from the relief Cushman cart and share a regimental smile, but then Judge Ridley, who owns his own caisson and cannon, marked the resemblance: "You have the cut of his jib, the hairline and crater eye sockets. Uncanny. You could be Old Jack himself. With the right uniform tunic, feathered hat and a horse, you'd lack only the beard to pass as Stonewall resurrected. You should take it on, give us all an inspiring reminder."

I have to confess, my vanity was aroused, all my dormant ambitions coaxed forward, the ham in me empowered, despite my wife's unbridled sarcasm. "You'd have to be something specific," she said, "before you could achieve the general." Nonetheless, for months the razor became a stranger. I'd scissor-trim with the famous "Winchester ambrotype" as my guide. Close copy, indeed, a twin, which Charlotte found foolish. She refused even to kiss me, but hard as I endeavored, I could never duplicate his signature icy glare.

Next season, I pulled a stock trailer behind my Endeavor and took the field as the manifestation of the man himself aboard a pied gelding I called Laurel. Sash and braid, field glasses and cold focus. It was a game, but a serious one, and I read deep into Robertson's biography to know which way to gesture and stand, how to phrase my prayers and when to unleash my anger. I could recite letters from his Mary Anna and elucidate textbook maneuvers, chapter and verse. Although some of the legend is apocryphal, I'd still suck the General's famous lemons to satisfy devotees in the gallery.

If Lee was our Arthur and Stuart a mad Lancelot, what was Jackson? I played him—though *played* scarcely cuts to the core of it—as pure fury at the sound of mortars roaring but bashful on bivouac as a bride. It struck my reverent comrades as too quirky, but my version of Jackson was divided as my own mind, which I admit has never been straightforward. I was living history. Are you getting this?

Charlotte, of course, achieved new summits of ridicule and scorn, and it wasn't long before she retreated into silence, swiftly followed by her absence and a writ or two. The savings, the house. That's a battle yet looming, and I should have seen it coming, however I was preoccupied. I protested that I was not clinically obsessed but merely in the throes of a passion, and it might pass. She could have ridden it out, indulged me, trusted to my previous history of benign stability, a provider and steady mate, but from frustration I grew weaker than my model and tippled to work up courage. When she left—and I suspect another, smoother historian was involved—I began to sample too much of the soldier's joy from the barrel, keg, flask or tumbler.

It was summer and miserable under that dignified wool tunic, but I had no classes to teach, an appetite for distraction and a war chest of bonded bourbon, so I surrendered to the tattoo of drums, the rattle of musketry and (spurred by the tune of Jack Daniel's best elixir) the soothing chorus of mating cicadas in the trees when I collapsed on my cot at the end of a time-travel day. I was fully drifting under the spell of Mars and the Cause, so it was no wonder I heard the voice. He came to me, he chose me, and who would be so heartless as to ignore such a summons? Some of you will surely understand.

It was in the tent I shared with Harvey Nevins that I first heard the whisper. Sweet-like, almost treacly. I was eating cush and hardtack, or to be honest, instant oatmeal and plain crackers; I do what I can to coincide with Secesh practice, but the lice and weevils some gung-ho Rebel actors adopt are further out than I can swim. Anyway, they were having a camp dance by the bonfire, and I could hear the music—banjos and fiddles, a squeezebox, mouth harp, Declan O'Somebody thumping the goatskin of his Irish drum—but it seemed too farb for me. All those wives, and a host of sightseers with six-packs and camcorders. The music has charms to tame us, and it was good stuff from *Fancy's Confederate Songbook,* but the rest of the whoop-te-do was pure distraction. I wanted to concentrate and learn the footnote details. I wanted hardcore. After all, this was the annual Wilderness Event with six thousand combatants, a colossal costume party and not a mile from where Stonewall fell.

I was reading, as usual, by candles ensconced in bayonets. *The Smoothbore Volley That Doomed the Confederacy.* It's half forensics, and by now I was so intoxicated by Jackson lore that I wanted to know where the wounds were exactly—entry, exit, ballistic secrets. I can guess what you're thinking, but I wasn't that far gone. No actual halo, no stigmata. I hope you auditors are still tuned in, however weird this sounds, as I'm moving to the heart of this matter.

I'd read and sip, sip and read, pour another tin cup of Black Jack. It was not rifled muskets that killed him, you know, but less modern weapons. That's half how they can trace what unit pulled the triggers. "Friendly fire." I don't care for that phrase, because frightened kin or friends are always the people who do you in, and when they do it, the fire is hostile, fevered, desperate, them against everything else in the world in that instant. It's not friendly, and the victims are no less dead for it being an accident. Poor Jack. Shots cracked from the shadows. Little Sorrel panicked and wheeled and bolted right toward the source of the volley. Later he was captured, as his master bled. As I said, poor Jack. Poor all of us. Only the sight of a whole corps on the ribboned-off field arising after the final whistle can offer any witness even temporary comfort from the notorious horrors of war.

Outside, they struck up "Cotton-Eyed Joe." Clapping, stamping, the shiver of a tambourine, and suddenly I began to feel light-headed in a way bonded alcohol doesn't muster. A tightness behind the eyes and a blood rush like I sensed something important was about to unfold.

Is there a term for an acoustic apparition? At first I suspected hallucination. Diet on the warpath is far from ideal, and I'd pushed myself on the march that day from south of Fredericksburg. High summer, merciless sun, and I'm not a young man anymore. The first words—chilly, more like breath than language—were, "Joshua Paxton, you're not me."

I was propped against the camp chest and facing the flap, so nobody was in there but me. I looked in a quick circle anyway, almost fast enough to give myself whiplash. Just two candles and random gear—blankets, mess tools, Harvey's red artillery kepi on top of its box fresh from Crazy Billy's Hats. Maybe, I thought, it was some joker outside whistling through the canvas, but before I could get on my feet, the noise came back, sharp as a razor. It was a Jacob Marley moment.

"I don't choose to take offense, Josh Paxton. I can see some persons might deem it an honor to be thus portrayed, but God's truth is I don't care one way or the other. I've come back to assign you a mission." No visual, no blurred world smell of spent matches, but the voice was mellowed by what must have been the grave.

Since then, he's given me instructions, signs and wonders. He promised I'd find a little white pine on the berm of the sunken road off the turnpike where the Chancellorsville affair concluded, and if I yanked it up and scraped my entrenching tool a few times, I'd find a spent Minié ball that passed through his wrist. This might sound foolish—I can imagine Charlotte's response—since a century and a half have passed. The site he designated is on the National Park reservation; in fact, that consecrated ground is just behind the information headquarters. It's off limits for anything but gawking. The earth may not be disturbed. I slunk out there, cautious, nervous, in an unfamiliar fever. The moon was big. I dug. The bullet was where he said, honest to God, and I became a believer.

You know the cadets at antebellum VMI did not accord him much respect. He was an awful teacher. "Natural science." Physics. If some greenhorn in class who hadn't heard the scuttlebutt dared ask Jackson a question, he'd go stiff as death for a minute, then loop back, begin the lesson again from the start, mechanical, verbatim. He had some technical expertise but no idea how to break it down as instruction. Behind his back, they'd sneer and call him "Tom Fool." He heard them, of course, but it caused him little despair. He loved God and his wife—both of them— and the sound of thunder. Still, they shouldn't have been so saucy. All in fun, some say, but the taunts were not wholly empty. Some might call it "friendly fire." You know how I feel about that.

He said to infiltrate just before change of the watch, to distract the guard, who would be eager for replacement and relief. Scout the terrain first, map it in the mind. Then strike like lightning and abscond by an unlikely path. Cavalry tactics, Stuart. Maybe I needed a silk-lined cape, an ostrich feather, but I'd cast my lot with Stonewall and aimed to be simple, bold and decisive. Once when I was grading tests in my office he came in and somehow blew the door shut. The legendary dead have their ways. He quoted Goethe, "Boldness has genius." I was in the hands of a master. "You can be whatever you resolve to be." He left me reciting the famous places—Rappahannock, Susquehanna, Shenandoah, Massanutten. He was a one-man campaign to make Indian names famous. He said not to hurt a soul.

I could hardly achieve the objective alone, but luck played a hand. I first encountered Aura Leigh (as I'll call her) in the Waffle House, which in Lexington is no bigger than a double-wide. I'd been at the Institute for Visitors' Day and toured the barracks, the Marshall Library and Museum, milling with the parents, lurking in the shadows, inconspicuous, despite the whiskers. Patches of snow pintoed the parade grass, and the brigade in full dyke and greatcoats had shown their moves. Friday, full dress. Manual of arms, bayonets. The bagpipes and fifes, brass band blasting "Shenandoah" and "Amazing Grace." Wind was whipping the colors horizontal and snapping like gunfire. It was all stirring, but I was shaping my plot. Singleness of purpose.

I had dallied in the museum, reconnoitering, taking mental measurements, weighing my task, so to speak. How many paces from here to there, how many shadows, how many ticks of the watch? Mapping and projecting, the imagination at full throttle until I was exhausted. Then I needed strong coffee and something rib-sticky, so I turned in at the yellow sign.

In the corner booth, she was propped back, head side-canted, eyes half shut so you could just make out the blue. Her red hair was crested like a cartoon woodpecker, and she was smoking so deep any bystander would think smoke was ocean air to her. Just a little motion from the neck up, but I could see the wire and knew she was i-Pod dreaming, lost in the music space like some of my students. Her plate was butt-strewn, ash blackening the yolky smear. Not a pretty sight. I passed her briskly and sat by the misted window.

In my booth I was sketching and figuring based on my reconnaissance. Among display cases, medals and swords, preserved uniforms and personal effects, I'd found the object of my inquiry standing in a miniature theater set, complete with strewn battle regalia and debris. Hitched to a post, as if he might shy and scamper, Little Sorrel was no longer a beauty, but still fourteen hands high—"large as life"—the color of chicken gravy, his glass eyes otherworldly and tail plucked thin by souvenir sneakers, his hide all scabby and peeling, muzzle grim in rictus. I found him the scruffy parody of life. He could once eat a ton of hay or live on cobs, and I knew I couldn't, not even with an accomplice, carry out such a contraption as he'd become. However, I was brainstorming, zeroing in on a stratagem. The lightbulb was coming on.

When I realized a shadow had fallen across the gluey pool of Mrs. Butterworth's on my plate, I looked up to see her standing there, taking a dragon drag from her filter tip. She looked me hard in the eye.

"I've seen you at the war games, dude. You're the man."

"Pardon?"

"Stonewall. You're the guy with like the horse and everything."

A shiver shot through me, and I leaned on my forearms to conceal my calculations. Even in mufti, I was a dead ringer to the trained eye.

"Aura Leigh, soiled dove," she said, offering a generously ringed hand. "I reenact a camp hussy. The enlisted man's second-best sexual friend. It's a hoot."

I couldn't help looking up, perusing the eyebrow piercing, nose stud, her cartoon Woody-bright hair. She was not my type of woman, but her voice had a familiar whispery quality I couldn't quite place.

"I wig up, take out the pins and hoops. You wouldn't know me. It's cool to play make-believe with people who are really into it deep. I like to play hard."

Anybody could see she was trouble, and I knew the general would disapprove—"He walks with speed who walks alone," he once wrote—but I sensed restlessness, daring, a prospect. And I would need a confederate, little c. "Accomplice," the bloodhounds now after us would say. And I should reiterate, Aura Leigh is not her name.

I won't say where her trailer is nor explain how we navigated the snowy roads. I really can't. I can, however, testify that the high carbohydrates of waffles and sausage don't set a good stage for midnight mugs of Wild Turkey, and I might as well confess: She has a birthmark on one nether cheek and a bluebird tattooed somewhere I won't say. Her private hair is wren brown, shaved to a heart shape, and she has learned her reenactment arts somewhere other than books. I woke just after dawn on Saturday to see her sprawled across the tattered patchwork quilt. She was still, like a designated casualty on the faux battlefield, hair the color of fake blood we use for a bad head wound, but her shoulders showed slight breathing, and she was snoring with a housecat's purr. It started to seem louder, though, as every noise echoed in my head like the bass drums of Friday's parade. I found the kitchen and a cup of cold water. Everything was a little too cold for comfort.

Aura had an old Dylan poster on one wall and on the other a big Kunstler print of gallant Forrest at a gallop. Her dental retainer lay on the bedside table like some weird mousetrap, but not much else testified to the trailer's occupant. She'd said she worked at a coffee shop, and she was quick and funny and seemed to be seeking a direction, an assignment in life. That was why I opened up, I guess. As my head cleared and the whole night played back on fast forward, I knew I'd said more than I should and done things not natural to me or excusable in Stonewall's code, but a partnership had been conceived and born. Despite my resolve to see it through, I wanted to be out before she stirred back to life.

Who knows what creates a girl like that? She'd matriculated to Hollins, where she'd written jigsaw poetry, made a film of hair in a drain and practiced what she called "recreational lesbianism." Then she bounced back to Lexington to seek her fortune in designer lattes and cappuccinos and work out her town-gown hostilities against Young Republicans. But she's tough and reminds me of Charlotte not one whit, so I took a shine to her far beyond the pleasures of conspiracy and Greco-sexual wrestling. I don't think that scoundrel Warr West would give her a second look, which raised her merit even further. I copied the number from her bedside phone.

"Thoughts black," the Bard wrote, "hands apt, drugs fit, and time agreeing; Confederate season, else no creature seeing." That passage kept ripping like lightning in my mind as I dropped her off on the assigned night to employ her gift for distraction on the security guard. When I asked how she'd manage, she answered, "You don't want to know," and her azure eyes beamed so sharp, even in the dark of the Endeavor, I knew she was right. "If my coat knew what I intended to do," Stonewall had told a subordinate, "I'd take it off and throw it aside."

On any night such a foray would be fraught with peril, but the local paper had announced that I had an ally of sheer serendipity, a local extravagant diversion. The neighboring campus of Washington and Lee was celebrating its favorite son Tom Wolfe, whose new novel on collegiate whisky and libido had sent his stock spiking. He was reading naughty passages in the elegant Lee Chapel, then planning to linger and sign copies of his blockbuster exposés of campus life. I knew the whole community—horse and foot—would convene to witness their aristocratic chronicler perform in his notorious Colonel Sanders suit, and from eight-thirty till ten, all eyes would turn to the wizard of trendy wit: He would become the town's center of gravity and light. What better opportunity to raid?

Two duffel bags, cobbler's snips, flashlight and a box cutter. Mute black clothes, no vintage regalia, just another swig to fortify me. This was wholly covert, undercover, no fanfare or banners flying. I knew the museum would be unlocked, as it is—in some martial code mysterious to me—pretty much a place of sanctuary and worship. Slink and scuttle, hush and creep.

The night before the caper the general's voice had chosen the kitchen kettle's steam for vehicle. "Ignore public opinion," he said, "if it interferes with your duty." Already the timbre was fading, going ghost-thin, but his tone was sure and emphatic. I knew I was placing my entire future in jeopardy. "The dead can rise and the risen can be put down. The most satisfying reward will surely follow," he said. They put his picture, after Chancellorsville, you know, on the biggest Rebel bill, the five hundred, but that was not what he meant. He was not alluding to dress-up theatrics or mastering any fidgety facts. I believe he had in mind a feeling akin to knowing you've behaved rightly and astonished everybody. He did not esteem strut or bluster, but was systematic as a multiplication table. I slipped through the door into the dimly lit Jackson Hall, down the stairs and into the museum with the uncompromised confidence of the righteous man.

You listeners may be shocked by what follows, ready to judge me halfwit or insane. Even as the authorities, no doubt, close in on this broadcast signal, I must reveal the secret, what I did for Dixie. Standing before the pitiful revenant, whom time had rendered similar to a camp mule in mid-bray, I petted Sorrel and whispered soothing phrases, reporting my orders, asking his forgiveness. When I uttered the general's name, I swear something in the grizzly animal almost quickened. He needed relief.

I snicked open my razor-bladed box cutter and made the first incision vertically from neck to brisket, then peeled the dry hide back like a field surgeon. Inside, as expected, I found no viscera nor machinery of life but the sawdust-filled burlap prop like the dummy burro in a manger scene. Then I changed to the leather snips and worked as fast as respect would allow. As soon as I had made my major cuts, I rolled the skin upward, leaving the hooves intact. Standing on a rickety Victorian ladder-back, I lifted the stiff skin as if I were liberating a desert mendicant from his ages-old hair shirt. The head, of course, was the hardest part, most delicate surgery, most arduous labor, done with tenderness. In just under an hour I had stripped the famous horse, halved the hide, stowed it in my duffels and was headed out the door. Relieved and feeling lucky, I looked back at the artificial shape of a horse still standing in his meager combat diorama. I was leaving VMI a crude piñata, and I harbored not one iota of regret.

In case you are inclined to doubt my story, I would offer this amber-irised marble the size of a golf ball. Anyone who has ever looked Stonewall's horse in the face would recognize its sad and placid surface, and if you examined it closely, you would comprehend why I had to undertake this whole assignment. You could see your own image floating deep in his eye.

I have no doubt my actions will arouse hot passions in your loyal commonwealth audience, and many will imagine me a monster, but if time permits—the machinery of law enforcement impending—I suggest you call in with any questions, for I am at peace knowing the noble steed's remains are, as I speak, being folded into the forgiving earth. Aura is efficient as an elf when she wishes to be, and I already count this mission a success. I ask only that you grant me some understanding.

After all, I have followed the chain of command, heeding the hero of Gaines Mill, Malvern Hill and Sharpsburg, not to mention his master-piece Chancellorsville, where he went out, though slowly, in full victori-ous glory. And I am ready to accept consequences, as even now I listen for the snare drum tapping "Rogue's March" and adjust my Hardee hat, my dress grays, the stars on my collar and my antique saber. I feel invigorated and pray the officers, when they arrive with their shackles, will handle me with the deference accorded a prisoner of war.

Plinking

Millard was out back practicing. He had hung his homemade "Gone Plinking" sign on the doorknob of the Swap Shop and was sitting on a sweetgum stump loading the tubes for his Ruger. It was a cheap piece of artillery, but the pump action allowed him to work fast with .22 shorts and leave any bystanders bedazzled. Rudeen had given up trying to keep him inside the shop on such sunny days, in spite of the way he enjoyed the restoration aspect of the job. His carnival years long behind him, he was still a local attraction, and he liked to stay sharp. "He's bad as a preacher," she'd say, "who's always got to be showing how saved he is. I reckon that's why he favors the kneeling position." She'd laugh her men-are-so-dopey laugh.

A company in Kentucky sold cards by the pound, all aces so you didn't have to buy regular decks and waste most of them. He would clip the fresh aces to the low clothesline in front of the mud barrow, then stroll back and pick up the rifle, which was akin to a toy in his humongous hands. Brow sweat would sparkle on a day like this, and he'd take a couple of minutes to get his breathing right.

When Jimmy Nichols came around the corner, he could already hear it: The Ruger spat and spat, the rimfire shells sounding like the sharp slap of fingers across a cupped palm. Shucking the slide without unsquinting, Millard shot fast enough that it resembled a measured and steady applause. He had popsicle sticks tacked to a two-by-four, and he split every one. He had red-dot targets you could obliterate with three or four shots so the paper never showed a trace of the dye. He did it in three. If he worked half an hour, he'd attract a row of local autodidacts smoking Camels and speculating on whether he had 20–10 vision or could sniff the heart of the target . . . or maybe he had made some dark bargain with the Choctaw griot man. But he was just getting started that Wednesday, popping the centers out of the aces, shooting alone for his own pleasure and that of God (who was, he liked to say, a qualified referee).

"You sumbitch," Jimmy called, and Millard turned, his gun catching the April sun. Jimmy shaded his eyes with his hand, like he was half saluting. "You sumbitch."

They had been running mates since before they were no taller than tractor tires. They'd married the sisters—Lurleen and Rudeen—pretty much on a lark. But the Swap Shop had come between them, and then the turkey shoots. No matter how hard Jimmy tried, he could not best Millard at sharpshooting. It was always close—a point here, another there— so it got to be a rivalry, then a feud. The blood ran hot at times, but in a friendly way, and they'd take up different corners at Jamboree Juke or a Legion Post social, spinning yarns on each other about as harmless as rolls of barbed wire. They had not spoken to each other beard-to-beard in the two years since Millard caught Jimmy fiddling with the firing pin of the expensive bolt-action Marlin he saved for the regional big-bore shoots. At least that was what Millard was sure Jimmy Nichols was working at.

"You sumbitch." Jimmy was moving faster now, not just walking but not quite at a run. Millard still wore the same puzzled look, as if bipedal velocity was the complication he least prepared for, as if Jimmy's voice had come back from some mythic land of mutehood. He could see that Jimmy was peeling off his wire-rims, stuffing them into his shirt pocket. Jimmy's face shone like a pickled beet.

It was about Lurleen, of course. She was the one who inherited the Cup 'N' Sup, which was a sight more elegant to operate than the Swap Shop. She was the one who held the Mary Kay parties and got the school board to forbid the teaching of the Harry Potter wizard books, the one with the toreador pants and blouses V-cut like they'd been split in the front with an axe. Lipstick the color of Naked Mountain merlot, fake fingernails curled like the talons of an owl. Even the geriatrics ogled her.

And local gossip was she was sweet on her husband's boyhood blood-brother. Rumor had it . . . well, it was a known fact Millard had been a sport when he was younger, but the fresh rumor was that she wanted to get back at Rudeen, because uppity as the restaurant business was, she wasn't raking in the cash like her younger sister. Because what Millard added to the Swap Shop was more than just being a handyman: He was an old-fashioned joiner, a true craftsman, some said an artist. In the evening or on days when rain plonked the shop's tin roof, he'd be at his bench under the bright work lights with a saw or drawknife, shaving rough spots off somebody's chifforobe, inscribing flower petals on a consignment vanity, pulling the bow out of a spruce plank. He was good with the razor and the oils and knew just how deep to sand when restoring an antique piece. He preferred to conduct his expertise in private, but it was known that he was a saint of the bevel and auger, the rasp and router. He could peg and pin, dovetail and mortise, and when he used nails at all—brads really—they were so fine that nobody could imagine how he could feel them in his huge hands. But everybody knew he could feel a trigger, could squeeze it so secretly and absorb the kick so well that only the crack of the powder and the jumping of some target downrange let anyone know he'd shot at all.

The story had it that Lurleen found him under the swag light, scent of the rosin in the scattered sawdust sharpened by the heat of the bulb, his face backlit in the same light—haloed, you might say. Rudeen was over in Macon on a buying trip, not due back till the late news. Millard was redeeming an Edwardian sofa for Burish Trapman, one of those foolish plush, curvy velvet-and-mahogany pieces that you knew had to be plum-purple and that only a prude librarian or an orangutan could find comfort on or admire. He had disappeared the dings with polymer and brought the finish back up with hand-sanding and stain. He was just completing the tapping in of the thousand or so breast-headed upholsterer's tacks when his sister-in-law appeared with the oldest mischief on her mind.

Theories about the specifics have since abounded, and even one detail of her couture or jewelry, his footwear or string tie or where the clock's arrows aimed, any smidgen of evidence at all was considered a pearl of great price in gossip parlors by the time talk grew general after Jimmy spoke to Millard for that first time in nearly two years.

Because, of course, Jimmy killed him. Shot him in the forehead, dead center, with a war-surplus .45 Browning, and Millard standing there with his plinking rifle in his hands. His *empty* plinking rifle, "not much more than a plaything," as Andy Arkwright said for the prosecution. The question of why Jimmy stripped off his glasses just before showing the weapon did puzzle everybody, but it was only his own testimony that brought that business into the case. Rudeen heard the shot and knew it was different, was not Millard popping bottle caps at thirty feet or cutting the edges off the lid of a soup can.

It's hard to say what will cause a man to snap. It's prone to happen in the spring, when the gusty wind carries the paper mill's chemical stink along the river and into town. Jimmy's lawyer opened by advancing another theory, the surprise of the trial. Sweetgum balls. They littered the yard like some ninja's playpretties, and it was just possible, barely possible Jimmy could've slid on one or two and lost his footing, possible he tripped and skidded and never aimed his equalizer pistol at all but just squeezed off a round as a reflex when his body tensed. Lawyer Holly Fenster, the most Elmer Fudd–looking man you will ever see, allowed as how Jimmy's initial intent was just to throw a scare. And he had a right to protect the sanctity of his marriage vows, after all. A weakness in all this, worm in the apple so to speak, was the beauty of the shot. It went in so clean and hot that nothing came out the front at all, not so much as an ooze. Of course, the exit wound—the sheriff called it that—in back did more than just part Millard's hair against the crown. What went in was no target load; what came out was a world.

I can't resist thinking of that last night at the Lessups': Rudeen already sawing logs in her French provincial twin, Millard at the window with the glass of peach brandy he allowed himself every night since his mother died. He looked after her, even when he was in the carnival—"living over the wheels," as he'd say, "with tiger tamers and bearded women." He'd send money; he'd catch a ride back from Galax or Monroeville or Opp. I remember bringing over some greens with ham two nights after old Miz Lessup expired in. Millard, no small man, was perched atop the kitchen counter, still in his funeral suit like some overgrown crow, and he had an awful voice, singing snippets of "Will the Circle Be Unbroken" over and again, and he'd sob, those heavy shoulders heaving, fingers gripping his temples like he was trying to force himself not to know.

So that last night before he died, Mill must've been savoring his snifter, looking out the window at the weird frenzy of the forsythia and the first white display of the Bradford pears, which would've looked ghostly and proud under the big moon. It was waning, just slightly after full. Still nearly round. Or he might have been watching the radio dials glow while he listened to oldies. He might have been going over his best grouping of shots for the day. He almost never used the human silhouette targets, but that day Sammy Poole had seen him hanging them on the pulley line. Some would tease a meaning out of that—Jimmy's lawyer, for instance, stroking his dome and asking the jury, "What was that Millard up to?"

He might have had the window open for the camellia smell. He liked to savor things. He was in the Masons and wore several of those symbol rings. He had a collection of antique tools—telescoping levels and fold-up rulers, wee bitty pliers made of brass. He liked to hold them up to the light, to feel in his fingers the exact nature of things, hinge and gear, calibration and sweet edge.

But he could also have been in the basement reloading shells. He didn't believe in waste. He had a bench with loaders, bins of shells, crimpers, wadding, sacks of powder (a mix he concocted from a book). He knew a fellow in Tallahassee who was running the Winchester powder shop: Fellow confessed to taking ginseng pills just to get it up. Millard didn't trust that, thought it might hex the bullets, so he made his own. Hardly anybody believes he'd go for Lurleen's sashay and shimmydimmy-doo, no matter what spangle or sweet nothings she'd come up with. I saw him once pulling whistlepig spines out of a stray redbone hound, keeping him calm with a soothy voice and holding him off from snapping while the spears came out. You could see he valued what he could do with his hands. Some things you can't believe he'd touch.

Lurleen, now she's always been a piece of work, always in a dance to music nobody else can hear. It like to made Jimmy crazy, that and his tiny, guaranteed flinch when the chips were down. Given the right encouragement, the man could screw up a free pass to Beulah Land. It was like a stutter in the nerves, but he was a fairly peaceful creature all the same. Usually. He'd learned to cook just enough to get bossy in the kitchen, spent just enough time over a hot stove to relish that bumper sticker: "Work is for men who don't know how to fish." The general opinion is that he was not devoted to the body for other than the culinary. That system of arranging your life does not guarantee a blissful partnership.

And Lurleen, well, she surely was a looker, and you had to reckon she had hungers of her own.

He sat vigil, cuffed to a deputy, with the body formerly Millard, and he wept. He talked to the body, private-like. Sometimes you could catch that he was trying to discuss ballistic stunts—the mirror shots, round-the-bend. In two-birds (he'd been known to tell this one when he'd had a couple of longnecks), you split your lead on an axe-blade to break two bottles at once. It was a cinch if you got your windage right. Then he'd commence to crying again or lean his ear toward Millard's mouth, like he was afraid Mill was taking the best bull's-eye secrets with him but might have a final word of advice.

What they came up with, the twelve gentlemen tried and true (though three were women), was a mix of temporary insanity and self-defense, followed by the anticlimax of probationary observation by a shrink, but right after the verdict Lurleen—who'd put on the dog for the trial, dolled up in black silk and a veil, her nails bright as cardinal crests—lit a skinny cigarette, turned to a weeping Rudeen, and said, "Sister, we done lost the hottest man we ever had." And then she smiled.

Nobody, least of all Lurleen Nichols, seemed to know Rudeen could shoot, let alone that she carried a chunky little Smith nine-millimeter in her bag. Looking into the dark, round, empty eye of that thing, Lurleen was the first on God's green earth to find it out, and nobody will ever know if she had time to be impressed. What happened next is why the Swap Shop is for sale this very day and why there's a memorial flower cross beside the courthouse steps and why everybody knows the governor of our great state, who is strong for the NRA but weak on snuffing a woman, has tossed between his gold satin sheets three nights running without getting so much as a wink. Yeah, she could shoot.

Stop the Rocket

From the first day of school, all the whisper talk was about the Rocket. Who was kissing who, the Blue Demons' lame single-wing attack, the dreamy new algebra teacher Miss Dauber with her saddle oxfords and silk blouse, even the polio scare—those topics rose, fell and dwindled on the buses, around the lunchtable and in the foggy locker room—but spooky speculation and hazed-over recollections of autumns past trained our attention on the annual appearance at the Spalding County Fair of E. J. Hippodrome Entertainment's most legendary ride. I didn't know anything about it myself. I had no notion it might show me my life.

Who can remember what it's like to be in seventh grade? You come in with your blue book bag, your gym shoes and lunch money. It's 1960, and you don't know if you're supposed to be collecting plastic replicas of Roy and Trigger or snickering over dirty pictures behind the Rexall. You wonder if voice change, whisker fringe and the circuslike sex drive are supposed to grab you by the throat or if you have to wait for some slow-motion Technicolor bomb to go off in your genes. You still want to flip spitballs at Stella Ray Prusey or play French legionnaires' last stand in the old Georgia Pacific caboose behind the switchyard with your running mates, but while you're thinking about smashing ripe pumpkins and filleting the frog in beginner science, your fast classmates are running toward the rough crowd, learning to smoke, talking dirty and bragging about how they plan to defy all caution and ride the Rocket till tattooed gypsies drag them off. The older boys with souped-up Chevies will show the way: They'll eat the wind and won't weep or heave or holler for it to stop; they'll ride that rogue rocket straight to hell. So they claim, and the talk itself can make your heart gallop.

Back then, my daddy was the best barber in Peach, and he loved to whistle "Summertime" or "Yellow Rose of Texas" while he ran the buzz clipper, snicked the scissors or dipped a comb in green Barbicide. He was a skinny cricket of a man with a Vincent Price mustache and quick fingers, an uneasy way of standing as if balanced on some tightrope in his mind. Smell of bay rum. Wire glasses. He gave the closest, hottest shave in town and kept his razor stropped to a legendary edge, but I didn't see how he could bear to look across the narrow Horton's Hair-and-Now shop six days a week and see his face getting progressively smaller in the dueling mirrors as he got older and balder with no adventures or wildness to break the rhythm of "Just a trim today?" and Billy Divine's latest salesman joke. Still, he was aware of a lot more than the small country of a barbershop.

He knew all those Peach men who worked at the bleachery or Dundee Mills and raised a corn crop or hogs, guinea hens or peanuts along with their own table vegetables. He knew the orchard folks who picked for Pomona or gathered pecans. He shared their gossip and hunting stories and fears, but although most of the adults in Peach were a quiet people, churchy, not sure they wanted to see the world in its deadly colors, they still loved the yearly fair and reveled in its green cotton candy and foot-longs, its cherry smash and candy apples that could break your teeth, the Tilt-a-Whirl and Screamer Coaster that whizzed and clanged around the field by the river sycamores where Hippodrome set up its ramshackle razzle-dazzle as if a tardy summer storm had blown it in by night behind the scent of fresh-cut hay. When Bob Renfro told the joke about the fair's animal waste shoveler or Steve Bridger mentioned the after-hours girls and winked, I noticed my daddy laughed hard with the others, his eyes crimped and glittering.

We didn't show any further interest, though, my family. Carter Horton was more likely to drive his tribe up to Atlanta for a pops concert or take us to the rim of the Blue Ridge around Helen to see the mountain leaf show, eat Talmadge ham and drink clean cider. Mild fun, sober. He might even take us to a cakewalk at the Masons or a garden show, but he did not love the fair, and I had begun to wonder if he was born too old to feel the thrill of anything wild.

But I didn't care. I mean, I hadn't known enough to. I was always too busy around harvest moon wondering whether I would be a wolfman or Crockett for Tricker Treat, but the year I hit junior high, I lost my immunity and caught the craze. I mean, just think of all the wild talk, people claiming you'd have to be one fearless man to ride that Rocket, have to be a tough fellow like Luke Tartwin or Junior Stemple, or plain crazy like Brudder Biggers. They said the laws of gravity would be suspended and you'd feel things like somebody in a waking dream. It went to your head like cheap wine, all that talk. Even a couple of high-school girls claimed to have survived flying in the Rocket, but I don't think they could produce a witness. It was almost exclusively a male ordeal, the space rocket to manhood, knighthood in the court of rusty, soaring steel.

The ride was a great old big thing, they said, taller than the courthouse, a radio tower-like structure with a short axle and one long arm with a rattling rocket car at each end. Back and forth it would swing, a huge lit pendulum against the sky, all its lights blinking and the screams like noises the damned will surely bark out after the Coming. They said nobody ever recalled what he had seen out the portholes, the sparkling panorama you went up on the Ferris for, the county stretched before you, the Flint River a dirty ribbon catching sunset, the people below like ants on a scavenger hunt. You were too busy saying your prayers. I kept trying to picture it, but I always saw the pendulum on our grandfather clock, and it didn't seem so scary, since it kind of paused or rested out on the end of every arc, but then I remembered the Edgar Poe story of the gears and wheels clacking and moaning as the big razor descended and the rats snacked on you. And when somebody told me the body of the Rocket twirled while it swooped, I felt goose-skin shiver my neck.

The rumor had sneaked around that some hot-rod pilot down in Valdosta or Rome had somehow come unbuckled and been joggled to death in the Rocket, but nobody had seen it written up in the *Constitution*, so it just upped the locker-room ante of brag and swagger.

Descriptions of the traveling folk who would show up one night to bolt the Rocket together and raise it and the rest of the booths and rides and tents by driving spikes into the earth sent even more of a chill down me. They sounded like pirates, and people said they swigged kickass while they worked and swore a blue streak, that they refused to wear gloves and would snarl at people if you looked at them wrong. But our neighbor Margie Larue told me they all had such honeycomb-drowsy voices and the deep coal eyes of swamp people, it was like they knew some secrets about the world and the runaway heart, and that drew you in like foxfire.

"You're not going, and that's it, so Katie-bar-the-door," Mother announced, but I knew if Daddy hadn't said it, it wasn't true yet. I was only beginning to grasp that they had a mysterious method of making a policy. All I could understand was that she had the first word while he had the last.

My running mates Brotherton Eisenhower (whom we called Be), Earl Dollarhyde and Starkey Waddell were planning to ride out with Earl's Uncle Banjo on Thursday night. I prayed my daddy wouldn't deny me the right to run hard with my pack, and here was the strange thing about him: He had this idea of justice that was more important than even what he wanted. He never raised his voice or sharpened his eyes when he thought somebody was off base. It was logic, he said, that had to rule our house. Logic and calm and the unsleeping quest for wisdom. After dinner, he gave me a close talking-to with a crumb of pie crust stuck just on the side of his mouth, hanging on the fringe of his mustache.

"It's exciting," he said. "I know it is, a giant pinball machine of a place, but it's full of dangers, hazards in the shadows, run by people we could not trust or respect. Shills and misfits, dead-end people. I don't mean to judge them sight unseen, but some things don't change, son. It pays to be wary.

"And I'm aware of all the he-man talk about that ride as the big test, so I know the kind of fellows who spit between their teeth and say they'll defy it. I was young once myself, you know, so I don't want you to feel you're under custody here or not trusted. I understand you're dying to go. You believe you need to, and that's a strong motivation, so I won't stand in your path, but you've got to promise me that you won't let any mob of boys, especially older boys who might have got their hands on a few ponies of Jax, shame you onto that Rocket. You can play on Sparky's Bumper Cars and ride the Mighty Carousel ponies or the Flume. Mirror Maze, OK; Clown Dunk, fine. A lot of what the posters advertise is just fool and foolishness. You can toss rings and pitch at bottles for Kewpies and see the stretch man, Tiny Bob, Herman the Human Torch and the whiskered woman. Not everything strange is dangerous. I'm not even worried about the Twin Ferris or the Screamer Coaster—I saw the pictures in the paper, too. But you must promise me . . ."—and here he reached into his pocket and pulled out a fresh five-dollar bill—". . . you will not use this gift from me personally to see a hoochy-kooch show or shoot a gallery rifle or ride the Rocket." As I reached for the money, he pulled it back a couple of inches and said, "Promise, you hear?"

Just at sunset Earl and I had ducked out of the 4-H chicken show tent, where we had mostly speculated on which roosters might be born fighters and how a whole egg passing through the vent never seemed to kill a hen, and we looked across the weird bazaar of the county fair and then up, up, till our necks cricked, to where the red and yellow lights along the Rocket's base and arm were just twinkling on like candy constellations. The place was a dazzle of barker voices, calliope pipes, sighs and cheers, the rattle and whip of the Tilt-a-Whirl and E. J. Hippodrome's Twin Ferris Wheels cutting huge zeroes against the gun-blue sky as the passengers let out a good-natured whoop and sigh. It was all gaudy tawdry, spiced with smells of chili and scorched popcorn, sawdust and the sickening appeal of spun sugar on paper cones. I wanted to hear my future from the voodoo woman Sister Mystery, and Earl was set on the music from the bandstand where Bubba Juke was just tuning their guitars, but we heard Be's voice calling out, "Y'all come watch me show the hair on my chest, buddies. I'm going to fly and spin like Flash Gordon, Master of the Purple Galaxy. Badass Rocket, here I come. Va-room!"

I don't much remember how they talked me around it. It was Earl who gave me the quarter so I wouldn't exactly break my word, and we got pushed to the front by a swarm of people before I could see the cheat in my reasoning. The operator locked the bar in front of us and slammed the hatch. I didn't see him really, but I smelled the fumes on his breath and the oil on his licorice-looking hair, and after that I shut my lids tight, which probably made it worse; the clanky rattle of chains reminded me of the cart in the Transylvania Castle, and the smell was gasoline exhaust like a drag strip. We couldn't've been slinging full tilt for more than two minutes before they realized I had been shaken free of my belt and launched against the seat in front, losing my dinner at every shake. They called it the Rocket, and I was surely seeing stars and comets and the quivery northern lights. It didn't help the way the brake or something stopped us quick and flung us again. When the awful motion stopped, I remember a bunch of hands reaching toward me in a blur.

Then the ambulance whipped its red light around us, and there was another streak of colored fire coming from inside me. I was strapped down but trying to throw up again, and everything went by the windows fast and swervy.

The pain wasn't the main thing, though. My lower arm bone was barely broken, a hairline crack. Before long I was wheeled into the lobby, where my father was coming through the glass door in argyle socks and matching vest. He was tapping a rolled up paper against his thigh as if he had a lapdog to punish. The pie crumb was gone.

As always, I had to have my radar on to detect the scald behind it when he spoke: "Well, Brooks, I guess it was just too much for you to resist. I should have realized. And you can't take the entire blame. After all, there's a whole crowd of yahoos out there, no doubt, some of them grown men, slapping backs and making dares. Of course, I don't know how many of them gave their word about it."

I wasn't even tempted to explain that his money hadn't come into play. All I wanted was to go home and retreat to my room, to slink down in the bed with my plastered arm angled in its sling like a deformed chickadee wing. But it wouldn't be that easy.

"You're the second boy today who has been in that emergency room from the Rocket, so it has to be stopped, and we're going out to the fair right now and see what we can do."

I was trying for invisibility as we walked through the thinning crowd, past the freak show, the candy apple stand and the Scrambler, toward where the Rocket was unloading its dozen or so passengers, who walked unsteadily away or leaned on the chain-link fence. I didn't want to look anybody in the face, so I remember a lot of shoes, most of them scarred brogans and scuffed Hush Puppies, a few frayed Converse tennis like my own. My father eased us through the crowd, who were mostly there only as spectators and had no intention of climbing aboard, and he opened the gate and walked through with me in tow.

"Wait till I get these people out, damn it." The man holding the hatch open fairly spat his words. "Can't you read the damned sign?"

He was a lanky, bronzed fellow with ropy neck muscles and a chestnut-sized Adam's apple. He wore black Levi's tucked into dirty white western boots. His khaki work shirt was drawn closed at the top by a string tie with a steer-head slide. Stitched above his heart pocket was the name *Coy* in leaning letters, and he had eyes like a water snake stuck into a face textured like a screen door. My impression was that he stood there coiled up, weight on the left leg like he was saving the right for something sudden and important. I thought he resembled a battle-worn Babylonian archer in my history book. Next to him in the flickering midway lights, my father looked like Mr. Peepers, and I knew there was no way any barber on earth could persuade this runaway from some distant world to change his mind, even about how much gravy goes on the grits.

"My name is Carter Horton, and this is my boy. A mishap on your ride broke his arm earlier this evening. The second injury today. This Rocket appears to have some safety problems, and perhaps we should consider getting it inspected in the light of day before somebody is terribly maimed."

"Says who?" This time he did spit, into the sawdust right between my father's shoes, which were coated with sawdust over their daily shine.

"I believe I just told you that. Carter Horton."

When the man reared back his head to bray, I could see both the nasty black spots in some of his teeth and the gold nuggets sparkling in others. But his laugh moved down to his throat as he leveled his face and then glared along his sharp nose at my father. The Babylonian was four or five inches taller, and his shoulders were broad. He was so weathered, not even Sister Mystery could have guessed his age in people years.

"And how will you plan to close it down?"

"I was hoping to bring you about to my view by reminding you how many people have been damaged. Children, mostly. I was hoping you'd call it a night and spend some time tomorrow looking to your buckles and bars. But if I have to, I'll just stand here in front of the gate, and people will understand."

The crowd was closing in and whispering, but I couldn't work out if they were taking a side. Then the man made a smile without showing any teeth. A smirk, I suppose you'd call it, and you could tell by his eyes that he was enjoying the whole scene.

"Well, I can tell you, Carter Horton, that you would be trespassing then. You would be preventing these good folks from their excitement, and that would piss me off. It ain't no secret that this feature of the show has bona fide popularity. Now step aside, asshole. I'm trying to make a living here."

That was what he said: "Asshole."

"No sir."

That was when the carnival man reached out with his dark, gnarled hands and took my father by the arms and slung him back so that he stumbled and fell into the fence but did not quite go down. His glasses flipped off somewhere, and I didn't know what would happen next. I couldn't imagine my father fighting, but I knew he wasn't likely to just quit, either. He recaptured his balance and stepped forward again, but as he got close to the gate, the man's arm shot out, his fist catching my father just under his left ear and knocking him into the oily sawdust.

I could see the crowd of hands again, this time reaching toward my father, as the men in their coveralls and khaki work clothes clustered around him, and I could suddenly hear Sheriff Clowsey's voice asking what was going on, then saying, "Stand back, stand back" with that air of command nothing but a badge can confer.

"What happened, Carter?"

But my father couldn't talk. You could see his jaw was wrong, turned a little cattywhompus, and he just glared at the man named Coy. Then somebody said, "This carny pushed Mr. Horton down and then punched him."

When the sheriff looked toward the dark man, he saw what we all did, a sneer. The carny couldn't have had more scorn in his face if he was a card-carrying demon.

"That right, mister?"

"Trespassing. He wouldn't let people get on the ride. He was trying to interfere with my operating a legal entertainment."

I didn't get to see much more, but the next day I heard it from everybody, especially Be and Earl. They all wanted my close-witness details of "the fight," which had evidently led to the man being carted off in cuffs and a padlock slapped on the entry gate to the Rocket. I had gone with Mr. Prusey and Stella Ray to rush my father to the hospital, and Uncle Banjo brought my mother in his truck. Daddy's jaw was broken. Most of the awful appearance was from it being whomped out of joint, but Doc Mutaspaugh straightened that right away, and he was sure the wire contraption would hold it back in place. Nothing he did stopped my mother crying and fussing, though, and once in a while she'd turn her hot eyes on me and glare. It was the Blame Look, and I'd seen it before.

When I got home from school, he was sitting at the Formica table, sipping Orange Up through a straw, and his face had bruised out purple as his prized hollyhocks. With the afternoon's flat light falling across his expression, he had a sadness about him I wasn't used to. His spectacles had cellophane tape around one of the hinges, and he was in his day-off blue shirt. He could talk a little and ask for things without moving his mouth, but he wasn't saying much. I figured he didn't have an appetite to traffic with the likes of me for the time being. Together, we must've looked quite a sight, though, him with his head bandaged around, and me with my cast arm slung in a diaper-looking bandage.

"He'll have to go to jail, won't he, Daddy? They'll all have to go away."

I wasn't sure if I wanted the fair disappeared like everything that had happened was erased or if I wanted everybody to pretend it had just been a meaningless scuffle. Did I want to be the boy whose father had shut down the legend? I was afraid I wouldn't have a life then, that people would shun me for being the cause of them losing something that marked the end of summer and drew boys into being men. On the other hand, I knew there was a wound in our house that wouldn't heal overnight.

My mother was wiping down the counter, and she stopped and gave me that Look Without Forgiveness. She was a corn-silk blonde and could go real scary-pale when she was on a tear. I knew she had wrath inside her and that only Daddy's soft words could bridle her back.

"Your father won't press charges. The man spent the night in jail, but he's out already, scot-free, probably having a laugh and a bottle of beer right now. The rides and the fair will go on, but that Rocket won't be lighting up and shooting back and forth, rattling people's brains in this town again. The Thaxton boy's family is talking about suing, and I'll just bet you those Hippodrome folks will be out of here lickety-split come Sunday morning. So the two of you did it: You shut it down. I expect some would be proud, but look at what it cost. Just look at yourselves."

Then he reached across the table and took my good elbow in his fingers, easy at first, comforting. I could almost hear the wire on his jaw vibrating when he spoke. "When you get healed, you'll have a garage to clean out and lots of hair to sweep up. I figure you owe me five dollars, son. I hope it was worth it."

When he wanted to be sarcastic, he had a habit of cutting his eyes to the side, as if confirming his message with some like-minded sidekick, but right then he was looking straight at me.

"In the meantime, I believe I've earned the right to sign your cast."

As he reached for the Parker in his breast pocket, his fingers tightened on my funny bone, and his touch didn't feel soothing anymore. It began to hurt as he squeezed, to steady his signature, I suppose, and looking into his jaybird-blue eyes, I was glad.

Visitation

Because I'm lanky my daddy calls me Goose, which is not a nice name for a girl, but he says I bring a dignity to it, so maybe that's OK. We will have an actual yard goose some day, he says, to go with our poults and foolish peafowl, but I am not holding my mortal breath, as he's mostly gone in the summer, off inspecting other people's cows for the state. We used to have a few cows ourselves, but Mama didn't take to them, on account of all the flies.

You'd never guess she and Meemaw was kin. Tonight, which is Saturday, just before something happens, the two of them are sitting on the lawn chairs just at dusk and looking like people from different tribes. Meemaw Ro—her true name is Juanita Butterfly Rollins—is in her blue-bird housedress cut from a McCall's pattern and having a sip. Her face is red as rhubarb, and a yellow turban covers what's left of her hair. What she drinks is lemonade, and she perches in that clam-back steel lawn chair stiff as in her pew. She is frail, but she won't admit to it. Mama, well, she drinks what she calls Tommy Collins, which I know for a fact is mostly Beefeater gin. Tomorrow is Sunday, and she will have to forgo, so she is having a tall one.

We sit out there after supper on Saturdays because the Moonbeam Drive-In across the street has no back fence, so we can see the picture shows for free—Alan Ladd, the Stooges, John Wayne in *The Wake of the Red Witch,* sometimes things with glamour women like Maureen O'Sullivan, who was also Tarzan's buck-naked Jane. Mama herself looks like one of those silver screen heroines in her flouncy blouse and black sheath skirt. Daddy told her once she was too haughty about her appearance and ought to ease off some. She gave him a look. Her name is Nell. She's a beauty operator. She can't drive the old pulpwood truck I'm climbing on, but Susie's daddy Croesus comes over and drives her to Bitty's Cuts, then brings it back till it's time to collect her. She is the one ladies go to for frosted ends, swirl curls, high style.

Now I am running around the yard catching fireflies to jewel my ear lobes. I like to tease the fice Dandy and listen to the crickets off in the stinky spirea bushes. Mama says I shouldn't sweat so; it's not right on a girl. Meemaw Ro says, "Let her be, Nell. It's summer."

My favorite thing about the outdoor movies is we can't hear the sound unless it's guns or a rock avalanche or Gorgo or something, so I get to be the story. I stand on the chinaberry stump pluffed up like a mockingbird and make the tale, which always begins "Once upon a time in a faraway place," because everything does happen in time, and it only happens once, and every place in the whole world that matters is far from this drowsy old town.

When I circle my running loops close to where they're sitting, I can hear the sounds of arguing, Meemaw Ro whispering and looking at Mama over her specs, Mama getting worked up again about how the coloreds should go back to Africa because they cause all our trouble, including Daddy having to travel. If he was here, she wouldn't be saying this, as Daddy doesn't hold with her views about race and how wrong the Confederate war was to set the slaves free. Right now she is saying that everybody has a place, and if they don't keep theirs, the whole world will be knocked back to the stony age. She is leaning forward, and her voice has a twist to it like sisal rope.

Daddy always says Mama has seen too much *Gone with the Wind* and calls her a "lost causer," but she is afraid of the Negro men down at Horton's Store and claims their women are always giving her the bad eye and fixing to sass her. "Negro" is not the word she uses. Myself, I like to run wild with Susie Day and watch her mama Harmony pluck chickens and roll out biscuits at the Step In, but now I would just like for the sun to finish falling so they'll hush up and I can tell a movie.

That is when I see a man on the road. We're the only house down here by the new stretch of hard tar edged on both sides with scrub pine and our feed corn lot, so it seems strange right off, a person we don't know ambling our way this time of evening. I can only see his outline for a spell, but he turns deliberate-like into the speckle-rock drive at our mailbox, and I can judge he is rough-looking and outside the circle of what I am used to.

"Rebecca," my mama calls me. "Come here to me." I scamper over, making like I just want to, but he is striding so long he almost catches up to my heels. The fice is barking yippy-yap, but when Meemaw Ro slaps her palms together and calls his name sharp, Dandy runs off under the abelia hedge.

He is darkish but still a white man, like somebody in the field a lot, with a straw hat and a rumpled jacket over his coveralls. His face looks like he has given up shaving for a few days, and by the porch light I can see a big scar slanting down his forehead and into one eyebrow. He has a wide nose and drilling brown eyes with big iron-looking hands. Breathing out a sigh, the man pushes his hat further back on his head and sticks one hand into a pocket. He shows what is almost a smile but is not.

"Evening, ladies. Fine place you got here."

I am standing right next to Mama, and I can see she is pulling into herself, getting small as possible and trembling. You can hear the ice rattling in her glass. She is wide-eye looking and breathing hard through her nose. The stranger is staring at her like something from Planet X. Now his lip has a curl to it that tells me he has already taken a disliking to us.

Meemaw Ro stands up then, stern and formal, brushing something invisible from her dress, her jaw tightening like it does, and she asks what she might do for him. The man looks over his shoulder across the yard, toward the car barn and the truck, then at the house, his eyes settling on the screen door under the porch where June bugs are circling the bulb or smacking the mesh.

"You see, I need to catch me a bus." His right shoe scuffs back and then forward again.

Before anybody can answer back to him, we all have to turn and look because the peacock is on the well house again, unfurling and making its ghost noise.

Meemaw Ro is the next one talking: "Then you need Horton's Store back the direction you came from yonder 'bout a mile. The public bus don't come this far down McIntosh Road unless it's the express to Jackson. You catch that downtown at the Greyhound sign. It's next to the Esso."

"Well, ma'am, that's the problem," he says, angling his head just enough to catch her eyes, then back toward the house.

"I'm just a traveling man kindly down on my luck. You see, I got near-bout no cash money, and I thought you might see your way to help me out." I can hear that, while he is asking for a favor and being neighbor-some, something else in his voice is not exactly asking.

That's when Mama pipes up, her voice nervous with trying to sound friendly, "Well, we might have some . . ."

"Nell, you know that's not for us to say." Then Meemaw Ro turns to me. I am stiff as a cedar post, my eyes wide and scared. I don't know what my mama's mama could expect me to do, but I can see everybody there on the outskirts of that pool of yellow porch light knows the edges of his words don't match their polite meanings.

"Goose," she says, which she has never called me before. I am staring plumb into her eyes, which are dark as blackberries with a look I do not recognize but understand that I am meant to follow like a code.

"Goose, you go in and wake your daddy from his nap."

"But Meemaw . . ."

"I know child, he's stormy when his nap gets interrupted, has been since he was a boy, but this man is needing to speak to him, and you know Roy Rollins is a man who will want to deal with it himself. You get along now."

Then I understand it is a bluff like in card games or a western. I see that the drive-in screen is just starting its popcorn and soda come-on, and I spin on my heels and dash off toward the house.

The man is suddenly bolting in the other direction just as soon as I take a step, and when I yank the screen open and yell "Daddy" real loud into the dark parlor, I can just see the stranger's coattails following him into the weeds across the road. His coat's cloth is split down the back like a mockingbird's tail, but he is not bringing a serenade to anybody here, as I switch on the parlor light and holler back, "He's coming. He's coming now."

Mama and Meemaw Ro are moving in my direction pretty brisk, and we spend the next fifteen minutes on the sofa waiting with the doors locked and the bird gun in Meemaw Ro's lap. Mama has made two more Tommy Collinses, and I have lemonade I am not drinking. When Sheriff Tesh finally steps onto the porch, I can see the fringe under the pink lampshades shaking with the weight of him.

The picture show for tonight is hopeless now, and with the sheriff gone they are arguing again, so I head off for Meemaw Ro's feather bed. The last thing I hear from my pillow is Mama's voice harsh like a rasp across the cutter bar: "A mulatto, I'm sure of it. He was just pretending to be white." I fall asleep listening for the peacock's shivery scream.

Shooting Booth

THE CONFESSION OF BOSTON CORBETT

I'm daft. I know it. All the sawbones say it, but what they mean by daft
is touched by God. Take up arms against a sea of troubles. It says that
somewhere in the Bible. He speaks to me, you know. I'll pass it on. I understand you may even be of the demon's party and in disguise, but you are
chosen to receive the tale. Even unto the Isles of Chittim and into Kedar
they would know of my fate and how I wore the avenger's mantle.

After the capture and his death, I signed the affidavit, and they gave
me sixteen hundred dollars, my share equal to the other troopers, but I
alone fired the shot. I was the chosen one, the one with the wound.

We had just reached Front Royal, horses lathered, us sleepy in the
McClellan saddles. Lieutenant Doherty said surround the barn, and we
did. One came out, the other dawdling back with a crutch. We could
make out his shadow. Just the two of them, and the twenty-six of us, all
veterans from the 16th New York, but he taunted us and spoke in fiendish
ways till torching the tobacco barn seemed to put him in his element.

Since the Gehenna at Andersonville called Camp Sumter Prison, God
had spoken to me directly. He said I was exchanged to bring the message
to troops on the front, so I stumped the camp and told of the she-dragon's
mission, her fetid breath. I chastised and blew the trumpet of the Lord
not to sow discord but because the Word was my fruit better than gold,
yea, than fine gold, and my revenue than choice silver. They called me the
Glory-to-God Man, but Christ walked in my tunic with me; I could feel
the wounds. I moved among the sons of man and raised my tongue for

Zion. When Butterfield blasphemed, I rebuked him, and they threw me in irons. My old injury flared, and dreams of garish women came. My sleep was a castle of screams.

It was memory retrieved me. Some brevet major recalled how I fought Mosby in the valley, snapping pistols till a dozen of his ghost men retreated. That polluted rebel mentioned my bravery in dispatches our scouts captured, so I had that sliver of celebrity and was set free.

Andersonville was akin to hell, our water downstream from the guards' latrines, maggots in the meager cush and only ragged shebangs to keep the Georgia sun from off our brains. Grayback lice, mosquitoes like sparrows, maggots. Despite the misery, I held my heart as a lamp and stooped to begging medicine and greens from a sentry, for better a living dog than a dead lion. I whispered gospel to those who perished and blessed their passage. The Secesh swapped me out because it was a poor-kept secret, how the rebel infidels were treating our boys, and since I looked hale and not a scarecrow, they thought I was one of a few who would give the lie to starvation rumors. I took the pardon pledge and broke it. I told all I had seen.

The curing burley caught like tinder, and the assassin was circled by fire the color of October leaves, though it was April. The smoke rose, and he stood in the door port with a crutch and rifle calling, "Give a lame man a chance." So he and I shared the misery of damage. Then I saw he lifted the weapon to answer our words, and that was when the voice came back, itself a thing of smoke and the thin light of dawn: "You must smite the unholy in his fire as he dances." It was familiar, a tone my father might have used when I was English and a boy. "Send him to his destiny now."

They say I shot with a revolver, but no man could have risen to that demanding a performance with a short gun. I used my carbine, and even then, I was off the mark. His shoulder was my target, but he moved, himself taking aim, a deadly thing yet, I now believe, and the lead went to his neck. One detective with us said the actor was a beauty in that moment, Apollo framed in flame. I know idolatry when I hear it. Newspapers proclaimed him the handsomest man in America, and since Ford's Theater, we all knew he was crazed, moved by some force beyond the human, the evil spawn. When I heard that voice, I knew the infernal was working through him, that he would rend the world.

I am not a good man, only a vessel. It is the hatter's madness makes me strange. The mercury in our felt treatment emits fumes that take us all by the mind and turn us peculiar. Grief complicated my situation. My dear wife Rachael died in giving birth near Troy, New York, and the daughter we would have called Cass went with her. I turned to strong drink and heard no voices to stay me, for I was still a vile man of the earth, a brother to dragons and a companion to owls, and when the two harborside doxies with soot in their laughter took me to their shed, I reveled with the brimstone drink. The words I told myself next morning were Old Testament: "Howl, O Heshbon, for all is spoiled."

You have to seek your own apt punishment, they say. I took the scissors —this was long before the war—and slit the bull sack, removed my two manly chestnuts in which the devil may reside, then went back to blocking hats with fury. And yet, I bled. Infection set in, and I suffered on the brink in Massachusetts General for weeks after. At odd moments the ache comes back, and it can rise to anguish, so I can never forget transgression, even if I am anointed. In the saddle I am forever in reminiscent pain.

We carried him under the apple tree, and Miss Lucinda Holloway, a local beauty, bathed his brow. We gave him brandy the color of dawn that was streaking the east, and he spoke, gasping, already a ghost. "Oh, kill me, kill me," he said, and, "Tell my mother I died for my country. I did what I thought was best." He wore no mustache, and I stood leaning against a tulip tree because I was tired and feared we all had made an error, but the voice makes no mistakes in mortal matters. That man was doomed and I the instrument only. God told me, "Rejoice, for you have broken the bow of Elam."

"Useless," he ended, "useless, useless," and that was it. Conger and Baker from the War Department rifled through his effects, the diary, the candle-splattered compass, penknife and pipe. Pictures of women fell out of his book, and I knew why he had been the devil's vessel and darling. The old stain, he carried it too. The harlots summoned him, and he answered. His end was written with a pen of iron and a point of diamond. I have heard his faithful, those struck by his passion on the stage, wore his hair in silver lockets. Woe unto them, for they shall suffer in the shadow of the scythe. Akin to scissors.

We were too far from the Rappahannock to hear the water glisten that morning, but something born of its shimmer washed over all us soldiers, and we knew the war had truly come to its final curtain and cost us Father Abraham's justice and our nation's soul. Booth lay upon a straw mattress, and apple blossoms drifted down on the slightest breeze. He looked peaceful, and somebody pinned his coat with a new rose, but not for pity.

The conspiracy frenzy was high, everybody wanting a target for the blame, so they arrested me shortly after, said I had to be in league with the others, deputized to silence the ringleader. I chafed in the chains, but God spoke how this was Babylon and I the emissary. "In due time," he said, and it was so. They released me and handed over a wallet of money. I knew I was no Judas. It was the same reward they gave my comrades. Duty to the flag and to His throne. I would not hang myself from the redbud's limbs.

"Glory be," I thought, and left the army.

They say I began to be a mystery, to move as an apparition, but it is not true, for I returned to Boston, the city I was called to like Paul to Antioch, and I set my weapons aside to resume the hatter's humble trade in the shop of Samuel Mason. Everywhere I stepped was filled with heathens and Jezebel women, so I spoke out with strife in my words and promised the tribes would swallow them up. The Lord would make that city a desolation and an hissing, but they painted me a fool and paid no heed.

New Jersey, Ohio—I wandered then, speaking my gospel of the New Covenant and the Second Coming, and some thought me mad, though you can see I've come full circle, as sane as a babe. And when I fell hungry and needed some of the ready cash, I showed my discharge papers and the portrait Brady's apprentice made. I wrote autographs for money. I raised my Ebenezer, then visited with Richard Thatcher, whose sweet acquaintance I had made in the stockade at Andersonville. One cold evening in that pit he showed me an ambrotype of his sister, and I told him they are all deceivers. Still, he saved me when I nearly crossed the deadline in a fever. The guards were only boys, but Wirtz had told them to shoot any man who strayed over that mark. Dick set me up with W. W. Garritt and Sons, so I sold patent medicine from a Conestoga briefly. It was not my calling. I was meant for lamentation.

Concordia, Kansas, became my wilderness, my site of trial. So as you see, there is no Seward in my story, no cabal or midnight legions. He had me released from the brig, but only from a distance. Conspiracy? They make me laugh. I was there in Virginia on military orders and God's blueprint, thus needed no self-seeker to guide my hand. I did not know when Lincoln passed that he would be a saint, yet I mourned him a prophet: We shared that. The coven they hanged in vengeance was poison enough to kill a king.

I lived in the dugout outside Concordia and shunned all contact with the weak sex. There I earned a reputation for shooting hawks and crows. I kept night-faced sheep and went to town only for provender, but it was '78 and Barnum came to me, offered to display me in a tent with Jenny Lind and the Feejee Mermaid. I read him scripture and said the curtain of his temple would be rent. General Tom Thumb and me, indeed! I am no ordinary gelding.

Despite Booth, it is Andersonville that has haunted me, the prisoners like so many lean kine in a pharaoh's dream. I learned to dry pemmican on the prairie and kept it in my boot so I would not be hungry again. I made my salves from forest plants and squaw recipes. This pilgrim had had his fill of men, as well, their lusts and rough talk, the addiction to swift fiddles and the scents of Sheba, but still the voice led me upon soapboxes to preach. They treated me roughly and would not heed the warnings. I took God's glory to the streets and was cast down, all to remind me of my transgressions. And when has a man worked out his salvation? I was anonymous again.

I sent a letter east to Booth's sister Asia, who was not the spinster I thought. She answered in calm words and said her family considered me their deliverer, as her brother's atrocities had to be stopped. She said I should have no regrets. Imagine. As if excuse from coy skirt-wearers were needed when divine instruction guides a man.

The GAR had it in mind I should be rescued. How strange that Lincoln, once so reviled by soldiers, would become their martyr and the amusing Booth the shibboleth. They obtained a post as an assistant gatekeeper that I might have a sinecure, and as always my handiwork with firearms was admired, for my eyes had not yet dimmed. Perhaps they thought I might protect their windy orators from other assassins. At least it was a chamber where no women ventured, though the statesmen embraced plagues and pestilence.

The story of my arrestment is exaggerated. I never fired a single shot that afternoon in Kansas, but only demonstrated with drawn weapons. No one stood in danger. It was a holiday, and the pages were performing their mock session for amusement, which did not trouble me until one preening jaybird mocked the prayer I myself had often been called upon to render when some veteran was assigning the day's offices. I will not hear God mocked. I thought to pistol-whip the whelp, but others dragged me down and wrapped my wrists in bootlace. I spoke of Migdol and Tahpanhes and reviled the golden calf, but they claimed I was only raging.

The Topeka asylum could not hold me a year. It was more Andersonville than you imagine, and the warden put me in mind of that German Swiss fellow Wirtz hanged as a war criminal for letting prisoners rot and starve. Some halfwit postman left a horse beside the entrance, and I was up and gone, just dust in their benighted eyes.

It was '88, and Booth himself only a rumor then, a bogeyman to frighten children. I went north, hoping the Lord would let his ice salve my sore groin. Minnesota. I lurked in the forests near the logging camp at Kettle. They needed venison, and I could still shoot. Half a decade I lived in a sod house underhill and spoke seldom to men or beasts. I was like unto a wild ass used to the wilderness that snuffeth up the wind at her pleasure. The voice came rarely, and then only to tell me I should stay safe in the bosom of the outland. When the Great Hinckley Fire struck in '94, I was wandering on a hunt, bringing down buck elk and salting them, caching till I could return with the wagon. I saw the billows of smoke greater than any tobacco barn and heard the rush of birds and creatures through the brush. Rehearsal for Apocalypse. I knew it was time again to move, though history says I stayed and became a cinder.

That was when I came here, and here is where I fell ill with the feeling of wool in my lungs. It's a smaller story than many would suppose and no secret. I thought to make a clean breast of my narrative to someone, dredge up the dregs, make my report, and you seem a kind and educated man. History is in us woven with our Creator's plan, and His Voice is the lodestone. Come closer and I will tell you the password for the Golden Kingdom. Closer still, to preserve my breath. It's Booth's, the last word, the key to paradise. "Useless." It rides the serpent's hiss, and why that is I will never be able to say. The harvest is past, the summer is ended and we are not any of us saved.

Acknowledgments

The author thanks the editors of the following journals, in which these stories were previously published: *Arkansas Review:* "Dear Six Belles,"; *Blackbird:* "Visitation"; *Crossroads:* "Bitterwolf" (as "Cherokee Killer"); *Gulf Coast:* "Razorhead the Axeman"; *Idaho Review:* "Trousseau"; *Missouri Review:* "Docent" and "I Have Lost My Right"; *Prairie Schooner:* "Stop the Rocket"; *Quarterly West:* "Shooting Booth: The Confession of Borton Corbett"; *Southern Review:* "Blaze," "Jesus Wept," "Plinking," and "Uke Rivers Delivers"; *Virginia Quarterly Review:* "Tube Rose"; *Zoetrope: All-Story* "Little Sorrel."

"Docent" was reprinted in *Best American Short Stories, 2004* and *New Stories from the South, 2004.* "I Have Lost My Right" was reprinted in *New Stories from the South, 2002.* "Jesus Wept" was reprinted in *Pushcart Prize XXX: Best of the Small Presses.*

The author would also like to express his appreciation for Speer Morgan, Ted Genoways, James Olney, John Easterly, Hilda Raz, Charles Frazier, Michael Ray, Sarah Kennedy, Kay Byer, Claudia Emerson, Kent Ipolito, Jeanine Stewart, Lee Smith, Bob Morgan, Ann Pancake, George Roupe, and the Virginia Commission for the Arts. And for his generosity and indispensable guidance with the manuscript, Michael Griffith.

The author also wishes to express his indebtedness to the following books: Clement Eaton's *Jefferson Davis* (Free Press), William J. Cooper's *Jefferson Davis, American* (Vintage), Felicity Allen's *Jefferson Davis: Unconquerable*

Heart (Missouri), Shelby Foote's *The Civil War: A Narrative* (Random House), James T. Robertson Jr.'s *Stonewall Jackson: The Man, the Soldier, the Legend* (Macmillan), Robert B. Krick's *The Smoothbore Volley that Doomed the Confederacy* (LSU), Henry Kyd Douglas's *I Rode with Stonewall* (Mockingbird), Richard B. McCaslin's *Lee in the Shadow of Washington* (LSU), Emory M. Thomas's *Robert E. Lee* (Norton), Charles Bracelen Flood's *Lee—the Last Years* (Mariner), Tony Horwitz's *Confederates in the Attic* (Vintage), Reid Mitchell's *Civil War Soldiers* (Viking), James Mooney's *History, Myths, and Sacred Formulas of the Cherokees* (Bright Mountain Books), Horace Kephart's *Our Southern Highlanders* (Tennessee), Michael W. Kauffman's *American Brutus: John Wilkes Booth and the Lincoln Conspiracy*, Sam R. Watkins's *Co. Aytch* (Simon & Schuster), James M. McPherson's *For Cause and Comrades* (Oxford), Jim Beloff's *The Ukulele: A Visual History* (Miller Freeman Books), and *Mary Chesnut's Civil War* edited by C. Vann Woodward (Yale).

R. T. SMITH's fiction has been published in *Best American Short Stories,* *New Stories from the South, Best American Mystery Stories,* and two Push-cart Prize anthologies. He is the author of thirteen volumes of poetry and has received the Library of Virginia Poetry Award. Raised in Georgia and North Carolina, he now lives in Rockbridge County, Virginia. He is the editor of *Shenandoah: The Washington and Lee University Review.*